THE SHADOW TRIALS

RITE WORLD: BLACKTHORN HUNTERS
ACADEMY BOOK 4

JULIANA HAYGERT

COPYRIGHT

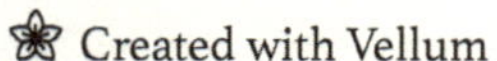 Created with Vellum

AUTHOR'S NOTE

I HOPE you enjoy reading *The Shadow Trials*!

DON'T FORGET to sign up for my Newsletter to find out about new releases, cover reveals, giveaways, and more!

If you want to see exclusive teasers, help me decide on covers, read excerpts, talk about books, etc, join my reader group on Facebook: Juliana's Club!

RITE WORLD

Welcome to the RITE WORLD!

Rite World:
The Vampire Heir (Book 1)
The Witch Queen (Book 2)
The Immortal Vow (Book 3)
The Warlock Lord (Book 4)
The Wolf Consort (Book 5)
The Crystal Rose (Book 6)
The Wolf Forsaken (Book 7)
The Fae Bound (Book 8)
The Blood Pact (Book 9)

Rite World: Blackthorn Hunters Academy
The Demons Kiss (Book 1)
The Hunter Secret (Book 2)
The Soul Bond (Book 3)
The Shadow Trials (Book 4)
The Immortal Vow (Book 5)

MAP

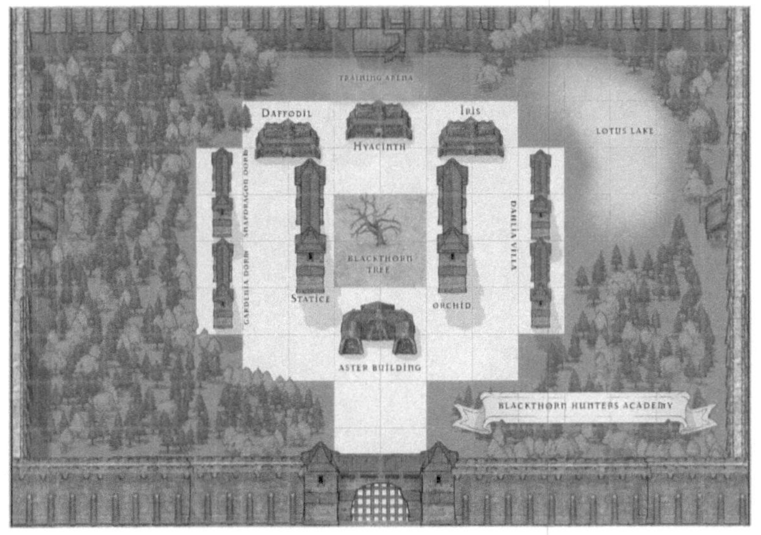

Map of Blackthorn Hunters Academy

Click here to view the map in a separate browser.

1

ERIN

With my hoodie pulled over my head, I sneaked out of the apartment.

Sneak might have been too strong of a word, as my mother wasn't in the apartment we had been sharing this winter break. In fact, she had been gone most nights.

During our dark magic training sessions, I wanted to ask her where she was going, what she was hiding from me, but since our relationship had always been tense, I was afraid that if I pushed her, she would hide even more things from me.

I stopped by the front door of the apartment building and glanced around before stepping out. It was early evening, and soon the sun would be down, bringing foul and evil things.

I wasn't afraid of muggers—I was sure I could take those if they tried something funny—but I couldn't say the same about demons.

Since my mother had been fired from the academy, she had decided not to live in Chasseur Ville, where all the retired demon hunters lived, because she thought we would be ostracized. Since she had admitted to teaching me dark magic and forbidden spells, and the fact that I had performed them, she was concerned that the residents of Chasseur Ville might not be welcoming.

So, she rented us an apartment in West Hill—the small town where I had gone on a date with Harvey and we ended up smuggling Farrah out of town during a demon hunter raid with Rey's help. West Hill was close to the Blackthorn Hunters Academy and Chasseur Ville, but the chances of meeting random demons were much higher.

My mother had found a witch to spell our apartment to make it harder for demons to find us. After all, I still had the damn mark on my wrist that branded me as the supreme demon's daughter, and that freaking mark called to demons. But once I was out of the apartment, the protection was gone.

But it was that, or I wouldn't see him.

Keeping my senses alert, I walked down the ice-covered street, turned the next left, then the next right, and halfway down the block, I went up the outside stairs bolted to rundown music store. The stairs ended at a red door.

I fished the keys from my pocket and unlocked the door.

Rey was in the middle of the empty living room, wearing only black sweatpants and doing push-ups.

Holy shit ...

My throat went dry, and a wave of heat coursed through my body.

Noticing my presence, Rey jumped up and smiled at me.

My heart skipped a beat.

This man ... a thin layer of sweat covered his ripped chest and stomach, making him glisten in the dim overhead light.

He reached for the towel on the floor, the lean muscles of his arms and shoulders flexing. As he dabbed his neck, his eyes locked on mine again. Those gray, almost silver eyes that could see inside my soul. His dirty blond hair was damp, making it look a little darker than it was. Strands stuck to his face, falling down to his sharp jaw. He ran the towel around his square chin, down his throat, across his chest.

By all that was holy, this man was so freaking hot.

And he was mine.

He was my soulmate. I didn't care that the soul bond was gone and we weren't connected anymore. Deep down, I knew Rey and I were meant to be together.

Rey's brows pinched. "Erin, what's wrong?"

"Nothing." I took my heavy coat and my hoodie off. It was cold outside and I felt the need to hide when I was sneaking around. I threw my hoodie on the floor and walked to Rey. "Nothing at all."

I rose on tiptoes, wound my arms around his neck, and planted a kiss on his chin. Rey hissed before snaking his hands around my waist, dipping into me, and covered my mouth with his.

Holy ... I melted into him, rather aroused by his musk scent mixed with his sweat.

"This wasn't why you came," he whispered against my mouth.

I bit his lower lip. "Can you blame me?"

With a groan, Rey wound his arms underneath my arms and knees. He picked me up and carried me to his bed, where we continued our game and got sweaty together.

I BURIED my face in Rey's neck, content and safe in his arms.

This had been our routine for the last two and a half months—since the school had been destroyed by Randall and we had been let out early for the semester. Every time my mother disappeared, I went to visit Rey in the apartment he rented, purposely close to mine. Our idea was to spend time together and practice, but usually our evenings began with us in bed. After that, Rey cooked or bought us dinner, and we would practice.

Then, he took me back to my apartment before sunrise, so I could be there when my mother arrived.

I rubbed my nose against his skin. Like this, in his arms, breathing in his delicious scent, feeling his hot body pressed to mine, I could pretend everything was perfect. We were normal people in our early twenties, getting to know each other, falling in love, and just living.

Not half-demons with a time bomb over our heads.

Rey splayed his fingers on my back, holding me tight against him. "It's getting late. We should start training."

"I don't want to. I want to stay like this forever."

"I do too." He pressed a gentle kiss to my shoulder. Just that simple touch sent a shiver down my spine. "But I don't want trouble with your mother. If I take you back and she's already there." He shook his head.

I pulled back and stared into his gray eyes. "Are you afraid of my mother?"

"No ... and yes," he said, serious. "I'm not afraid of her as a person, or a demon hunter, but she's your mother. I don't want to give her more reason to not like me."

I frowned. For almost a year, Rey had struggled with his feelings for me. In his mind, the honorable thing to do, and to keep me safe from the dangers surrounding him, was to stay away from me. On top of that, my mother had warned him off. But then, right when everything fell apart last semester, my mother told Rey to ignore whatever she had said and protect me. According to him, that wasn't why he finally surrendered to his feelings, but he said it certainly lifted some of the pressure.

However, ever since then, my mother didn't seem keen on my relationship with Rey. Of course, she knew what was going on—she wasn't stupid—but now that things had settled down, I felt like she wanted to take back what she told him. She wanted to tell him to keep his hands off me again, but she also knew it wouldn't work this time.

I wouldn't let it work.

"I don't care what she thinks about our relationship," I said, my voice low. "All I care is how we feel about each other."

One corner of Rey's lips curled up before he leaned in and kissed me. A deep but brief kiss that left me breathless. "Come on," he said, getting up from the bed. "I have leftovers from yesterday's pasta."

He pulled on his sweatpants and put on a black shirt. And I pouted as he trudged to the kitchen. Seriously, I got it. We had to get out of the bed at some point.

But did he need to put a shirt on?

Sighing, I rolled to my side and got up. While Rey fixed us dinner, I put my jeans and blouse back on. I glanced around, making sure I hadn't forgotten anything. But there was no place to hide things here.

This apartment had a large open floor plan, with a few archways that marked the bedroom, the kitchen, and the living and dining areas. The only thing separated by a door and walls was the bathroom. Rey had rented this place because it was close to the apartment my mother had rented, and because it was large and we could practice in here without much trouble. Because this wasn't a normal apartment, he didn't even try to buy furniture for it. Only a king-sized bed for the bedroom, and two stools for the kitchen island. And also bedroom and kitchen stuff—sheets, pillows, and blanket, and a few pots and pans, plates, and cutlery.

I dragged my bare feet across the old hardwood floor to the kitchen. Rey was reheating the sauce in a small pot on the range. I halted behind him, wound my arms around his waist, and rested my cheek on his back. The *thump-thump* of his heart was strong in my ears.

"What is it?" he asked, bringing one of his hands over mine.

I shrugged. "Just ... whenever I'm here with you, like this, I can pretend we're human."

Rey let go of the sauce and turned to me. "We might not be regular people, but we're together, and we'll be together forever. We'll overcome anything that comes our way." He placed a soft peck on my forehead. "Now help me." He slapped my ass. "Get the plates and such."

I groaned, but relented. I set up the island with plates, forks, and knives, and glasses with water. A minute later, Rey brought over the rose alfredo fettuccine he had whipped up last night—it had been incredible. Who knew my half-demon could cook?

After we ate and cleaned up, Rey and I relocated to the empty space in the loft.

Rolling my shoulders, I faced him. "So, what will it be today?"

"As much as I would love to move on to more complex spells, I think we need to continue practicing teleporting."

I nodded. During my mother's training sessions, we practiced dark magic—syphoning energy from dead bodies, reanimating them, among other things. With Rey, I trained in sword combat, so I would not get rusty, but the main focus of our sessions was my demon powers. When we first started, Rey told me that each demon had different powers and abilities. Most of them originated from dark magic, but depending on the demon ranking and affiliation, the range of powers changed.

Since I was the daughter of the supreme demon, he thought my powers were unmatched, and he wanted to see what I could do.

So far, I hadn't been able to do much.

But there was one spell I really liked, though I still hadn't gotten the hang of it: teleporting.

"All right," I said, shaking and loosening my arms. Teleporting was fine in theory, but in practice, it could get messy.

I breathed deeply and channeled my magic. The power filled my veins and ignited my core instantly. I focused and visualized myself on the other side of the room.

I blinked and—

The world shimmered before my eyes, a dark veil fell over me, pressure started in my ears.

And I moved a foot forward.

"Holy shit," I mumbled.

"It's okay." Rey approached me. He held my hands. "It's the same thing every night. You're trying too hard. We already know you can do it. Now, you just have to let your instinct take over."

I wished it was that simple. When we first attempted this ability, Rey told me most demons could not teleport. At first, he thought that, as a half-demon, I wouldn't be able to do it.

He couldn't, though I learned he could shift into a cool raven —he had been the one I had seen outside the Gardenia building so many times. He had admitted to following me to make sure I was okay. It was one more thing to prove that he really loved me, but had held on to what he thought was right.

However, when we were first recruiting half-demons for Randall's Black Knight Unit, we had seen Zachary teleport, so Rey thought I could do it too. After telling me his theory and practicing it with me, Rey simply called the shots.

The first few tries, I didn't do anything. No shimmering lights, no pressure, no underwater feeling. But then it happened. I felt the whoosh of air across my face, and I had moved an inch.

I guess a foot was better, but it was still not enough.

"We've been practicing this for two months," I said, feeling completely frustrated. "So, for me to actually appear on the other side of the room, it will take how long? Two years?"

Rey squeezed my hands. "I'm sure you're having a hard time because this is still new. And, like I said, you're being too hard on yourself. Once you unlock the mystery, you'll be able to teleport two feet or two hundred as if it was the same thing."

I wanted to stomp my feet and pout and yell that this was useless, but I reined in my tantrum. Having these crazy fits wouldn't help me, but it would be great if I could make some progress soon. In a week, we were going back to the academy for the new semester, and I would feel better if I had a handle on this spell before classes started.

I rolled my shoulders again. "Okay, okay. Let's try again."

"That's my girl." Rey leaned into me and place a quick kiss on my lips before stepping back.

I frowned at him. "That doesn't help."

"What doesn't help?"

"Calling me my girl and kissing me all the time," I said. "All that does is make me want to jump your bones."

Straightening, Rey cleared his throat. "As much as I like that idea, I think we have to use the time we have left to practice."

I was of the opinion that we could use that time to stay in bed, tangled with each other. Once we were back at the academy, we would have to pretend to be student and professor again. If someone saw us together, Rey would be fired, and I would be in hot water, and since I was always in hot water, it would be best if we lie low.

Damn, that would be so freaking hard.

I let out a long breath. "All right, all right. Let's give this another try."

I closed my eyes, channeled my magic, and—

A knock came from the door.

Rey and I stared at each other. No one knew where Rey was hiding besides me, and I had the keys to enter without knocking.

"Are you expecting someone?" I asked.

Rey shook his head.

The knock came again.

Tense, Rey went to the door. He pressed his ear to the wood. A moment later, he opened the door an inch.

A white piece of paper flew through the crack and landed right at my feet.

Rey opened the door wider, but there was no one there. "What the fuck?" I crouched down and picked up the paper

—it was an envelope. Rey quickly closed and locked the door, and came to my side. "What's that?"

"A letter," I whispered as I pulled out the note from inside the envelope. I gasped as I read it. "It's from Tanner." I glanced up at Rey. "He wants us to meet him."

ERIN WANTED to leave right away, but I hesitated. How the fuck had Tanner found us, and how had he sent the letter like that? Was he working with a witch, or something?

I couldn't deny, though, that I had thought about Tanner a few times in the past couple of months. We hadn't heard from him since he faked his death, revealed he was Erin's half-brother, and disappeared from the academy.

I was curious about what he had to say.

After a little discussion about how to better respond to the letter, Erin and I decided to meet him. We left my loft, got my car from the parking lot across the street, and drove to the meeting place written on the note.

On the way, I glanced at Erin. She stared out the window, a hint of smile on her lips. Other than when we were just being a couple, I hadn't seen her smile in months. She was always worried about what would happen next. How would the academy be when we went back? How would Crimson be as the new headmaster? How could she find the other two Demon Kissed Queens? When would she have total control over her powers? When would Brikan finally make his move and come for her?

I didn't tell her, but those same questions kept me up at night—or day, since I only slept once she left and went back to the apartment she shared with her mother.

When Erin wasn't with me, I researched. Sometimes, I shifted into my raven and flew to other towns and cities, trying to find a clue, anything, that pointed to how and where we could find Erin's half-siblings. No spell I knew or had heard of worked. Soon, I would hunt down witches to find a specific spell that could help us.

It wasn't a bad idea, but I didn't want to risk having witches after us, and starting another war.

I glanced at Erin again. With that smile, she looked serene, and that made my heart flutter. Erin made my heart flutter often. She was beautiful—long black hair and bright golden eyes, and hot with her lean and hard body. Whenever she touched me, she rubbed her body on mine, whenever we made love ... I sucked in a sharp breath, wondering if we would be done with this quickly, so I could take her back to my apartment.

But more than anything, Erin was everything I ever wanted. She was a good friend, had a big heart, and always tried to do what was right. Like any person, she had her moments when she chose the wrong route, but once she realized she was wrong, she tried to correct it.

To me, Erin was perfect. She was everything. She was my heart and soul.

In the past two months, I had told her I loved her a bunch of times, but I wasn't sure she grasped how much. If something happened to her, if her father succeeded ...

I tightened my grip on the steering wheel until my knuckles turned white.

"Everything okay?" Erin asked, her voice sweet.

I glanced at her, at the faint smile on her lips, and the brightness of her eyes. How could I hang on to anger and anxiety when she looked at me that way?

"Just curious about what Tanner will tell us," I said, which was true.

"Me too," she whispered.

Following Tanner's instructions, I turned my car onto a dirt road outside of town, now covered in a thin layer of ice. A minute later, we spotted a truck parked between some snow-covered trees. We parked right beside it and left the car on, so the headlights would illuminate the place in the darkness. We hopped out of my car and sank our feet into the soft snow.

Tanner appeared from the shadows.

The tall guy didn't resemble Erin at all. The only thing the siblings had in common was the color of their hair—black. While Erin's was straight as a board, Tanner had a mop of bouncy curls atop his head.

Tanner raised a hand in greeting. "Long time no see."

"Long time and no news," I said, my voice flat. Even though it was good to finally hear from him, he had been gone awhile. Anything could have happened in the meantime.

"Hi, Tanner," Erin said.

"I'm hoping I didn't startle you with my letter," Tanner said. "It's a trick I learned from some witches a couple of months ago."

"Neat trick." I halted a few feet from the guy, right beside Erin. "So, care to tell us what you've been doing all this time?"

"That's why I called you here," Tanner said, his dark eyes narrowing. "I've been following trails and jumping from town to town, trying to find more about the prophecy. Unfortunately, most supernaturals aren't very open to a half-demon, half-demon hunter combo, so my research has been messy." He cringed, probably remembering some gruesome situation he had gone through.

"Did you find anything?" Erin asked, her voice full of hope.

"I didn't find anything about the prophecy's wording, like I wanted, but I did find out who made the prophecy," he said. "Her name is Fiona, and she's a witch from an extremely ancient and powerful line."

Erin's breath caught. "Where is she?"

"That's the thing. I don't know," Tanner said, dejected. "I couldn't even find out what coven she is from. All I know is that she's in hiding now."

"Shit," Erin muttered. She glanced at the mark on her wrist. "Only she can tell me about this, why there are only three Demon Kissed Queens, when King Brikan has hundreds of children, why I'm one of them, and what the hell this means." She lifted her eyes to Tanner. "We really need to find her."

"I agree, but how do you find a witch who is in hiding?" Tanner asked.

"You have no clues?" I asked, still wary.

Tanner shook his head. "My plan is to search for her now, but I don't know how long that will take."

I wanted to tell him we would help him, but with classes starting again in a week, there was no way. And Erin and I already had our hands full trying to locate their other half-siblings.

I nodded. "Do that. Let us know if you need any assistance."

"I will," Tanner said. He stared at Erin. "Take care, sis."

Erin's eyes went wide. She was so stunned with the nickname that she didn't say anything as Tanner hopped in his truck and drove away.

"He called me sis," she whispered once he was gone.

"Well, he is your brother."

She turned those big, bright eyes to me. "I guess I had realized that, but this is the first time I actually felt something." She rested a hand over her heart. "I never thought about having siblings, and now I have hundreds. If this situation wasn't so dreary, this would be funny."

I went to her and slipped my hands in hers. "Are you ready for this? Searching for your siblings and meeting them?"

"Yes. No." Erin let out a long sigh. "I don't know. I mean, do I have a choice? I'll need them if we want to defeat Brikan."

I frowned. Even if all demon hunters and half-demons gathered to fight the supreme demon, I still wasn't sure we would succeed. But I didn't mention that, because I had hope. I had hope we would, somehow, kill him. And then Erin would be safe. That was all that mattered to me.

I tugged at her hands, pulling her to me. "It'll be okay, Erin. I'll be right beside you, and I'll never let anything happen to you."

She scoffed, but then showed me a small smile. "I wish you were that powerful. Then you could just walk into the underworld, take my father down, and we wouldn't have to agonize over this." She rose on her tiptoes and pressed her lips to mine. "Thank you, though. For sticking with me."

"Anything for you," I whispered before dipping into her and turning that tease of a kiss into a real one. I pressed her to the side of my car, trapping her against me.

She clung to me while I devoured her delicious mouth and drank in her sweet rose scent. I knew that she would totally be onboard if I laid her down on the backseat and took her right here, right now.

But it was too fucking cold here.

So, I did the next best thing.

I broke the kiss, opened the car's door, helped her inside, and said, "We can continue that once we get back to my loft."

Faint red tinted her cheeks, but she didn't avert her gaze.

I slammed the door shut before I reconsidered my plan. Then, I raced to the other side of the car so we could get out of there.

3

ONE DAY before classes officially started, my mother drove me back to the academy. I wished I could have come with Rey, but now that he was my professor, it would be suspicious.

However, my mother didn't drive inside the gates, as Crimson had not only upheld Randall's wishes of having her fired, but he also forbade her from entering the grounds.

So, she parked her car outside the gates, while all the other students went inside.

I grunted. "This is going to be ridiculous."

"What will?" she asked, her hazel eyes narrowed.

"Having to walk down the road to the Aster building, holding my bags."

She nodded. "I'm sorry about that. If I could, I would come in with you and help you with your stuff."

She had never helped me with it before. Why start now?

A week had passed since Rey and I had seen Tanner, and my mother had gone missing during the night. After that, she had been out twice more. When I tried touching the subject the next day, she always shut me down. If she had hopes of someday salvaging our messy relationship, she was doing a poor job.

But I didn't push it. She was hiding things from me, and I hid things from her. If I insisted on being a part of whatever she was plotting, then she would demand to know what I knew, and I wasn't ready to share my plans.

I let out a long sigh and reached for the door.

"Erin, wait." My mother's hand closed around my wrist. "Please, be careful. Things will probably be even worse this semester, and who knows what Crimson is up to. And since I won't be there to protect—"

"I thought you told Rey to protect me," I said, hitting that button on purpose.

My mother pressed her lips into a thin line. "Holy sh—" She stopped herself. "You know how I feel about you and Rey, and—"

"And you know how we feel about each other," I said, interrupting her again. "I know you told him to forget your warning and protect me because, at that moment, you saw no other way. You didn't know what would happen once you were escorted out of the academy. I get that. But, please, try to understand. Rey and I ..." I sighed. My mother didn't know Rey and I had once shared the soul bond. If she knew, she would certainly freak out. I went on, "We love each other, and nothing will change that."

She shook her head. "At least I know he'll do everything in his power to keep you safe."

I patted her hand, then disentangled it from around my wrist. "It'll be okay. I'll be okay."

I could see the anguish stamped in her eyes, and it killed me that besides saying, "be careful," she didn't say more. She never touched on anything below the surface—how she felt, her hopes, her dreams, her fears.

"All right," I said, finally opening the door. "I'm off."

"Call me later!" She leaned over the passenger seat so that she could look at me. "I know you have your phone with you, so call me every day. Understand?"

I rolled my eyes, feeling like a teenager. "Yes, ma'am."

I got it that the demon hunter society was different. While humans at my age were considered adults, going to college and living their own lives, demon hunters still lived in a private school of sorts, and their parents still had too much say in their lives.

Pushing those thoughts away, I stepped back and closed the door. "Bye," I mouthed. Then, I grabbed my bags from the trunk and marched past the gates.

Here, the snow had been cleared from the road and the path, making it less likely I would slip and fall on my face. But the cold radiated the same. Fighting with my bags, I zipped up my thick jacket.

This was probably the first time I had walked into the academy on foot, and right now, I felt like a small ant facing a giant. In the distance, the Aster building rose high, with its gray stones crawling with dark vines and black thorns. From the entrance road, no one could see the rest of the academy, behind the main building, had been destroyed. I was curious to see how everything looked now.

Had they remodeled the academy, or was it the same?

Since it hadn't been affected, the Aster building was still the same. If I squinted, I could believe it was a haunted house.

An amused chuckle rose past my throat. It had been a dare and a haunted house that had put me on this path.

Would I be here if I hadn't gone in that house? Would my aunt be alive? Would King Brikan be after me?

Would I have met Rey?

I shook my head. No, I couldn't think about that. What was done was done. With the exception of what happened to my aunt, I didn't regret anything. Well, maybe bullying Rey into breaking the soul bond, so he would confess, but even that was okay now. We were together, and we would face whatever came for us together.

I hiked the strap of one of my duffel bags higher on my shoulders, just as a sedan rolled to a stop beside me. I steeled myself, ready to ignore the dumbasses who would tease me, call me mongrel, or worse.

But to my surprise, I heard a squeal. "Erin!"

I gasped and turned, staring right into my best friend's green eyes. "Claire!"

"Hop in," she said with a wide smile. "I'll take you the rest of the way."

It seemed silly to get a ride halfway, since both of us would have to walk from the underground garage to the dorms, but I was relieved. This walking thing seemed too much like a walk of shame. I had never had one of those before, and I didn't want to start now.

I threw my bags in the backseat and slipped into the passenger seat. The moment I closed the door, Claire threw herself at me and pulled me into a bear hug.

"Holy crap, I missed you," she said.

Chuckling, I hugged her back. "We spoke."

She pulled back. "Yeah, but I didn't see that pretty face of yours in so long. And, incredibly, I stayed out of trouble for just as long. Boring!"

I chuckled again. Only she could make me feel good

about coming back to a place that I both loved and hated so much. But this was my home, in a way. The only home I had and wanted.

Unless Rey bought us a chalet at the edge of a lake and wanted to disappear with me. Then, yeah, that would definitely be my home.

Claire drove again.

"So, tell me, how was the family vacation?"

Claire wrinkled her nose. "Terrible." To Claire's dismay, her father had taken her and her grandmother to their beach house in California. Before going, she told me it was a big, beachfront house, and if it weren't for the fact that she had to endure her father and her grandmother, the place and the scenery would actually be amazing. "Though, the three weeks we were there, my father was only with us for a couple of days."

"Why is that?"

Claire maneuvered the car into the garage and into her reserved parking spot. "He said he had to check on the academy's reconstruction." She shrugged. "Not sure I believe him."

I frowned. During the longer break, Rey had told me he had a made a fast verbal deal with Professor Crimson, asking him to stop the upcoming Shadow Trials. Crimson had promised he would put an end to the deadly contest once they succeeded, but Crimson had gone back on his word. Rey said he always knew Crimson wasn't to be trusted, but now he was suspicious the new headmaster was plain evil—just like Randall had been.

Once she turned off the car, Claire turned to me. "So, tell me, how are things with Rey?"

I smiled at her. "Perfect."

I opened the car door, but Claire grabbed my arm. "Come on, I want more details," she whined.

I shooed her away. "Nope. That's between him and me."

We got out of the car and picked up our bags, just as new cars entered the garage. Remembering what had happened last semester, I ushered Claire to the stairs.

"Let's get out of here before I start the first day by breaking someone's nose."

Claire lifted a finger. "Ha, see, that's what I missed."

I shook my head as we raced up the stairs to the main level.

I halted as soon as the rest of the academy came into view.

The courtyard with the Blackthorn tree, and around it the Statice, Orchid, Iris, and Daffodil buildings.

It was exactly the same. The academy had been rebuilt to look exactly the same, from before Randall destroyed it. However, now the buildings' gray stones were lighter, or cleaner and less old, and the flowerbeds flanking the snow-cleared paths were empty.

For some reason, I had expected to notice a bigger differ-ence. With the new headmaster calling the shots, I actually believed he would make it all different, as if he wanted to erase Randall's existence and legacy from our history.

"I know, I'm shocked too," Claire said from my side. Like me, she stared at every single detail. "I really thought he would take advantage of this to tear everything down and build something more modern."

"I'm glad that isn't the case," I said. I liked this place just the way it was.

Claire nudged my arm. "We better go and get ready. I know my father will be assembling everyone later."

I frowned. "For?"

"His first speech as the new headmaster."

<hr>

CLAIRE HAD EXPLAINED to me that the new headmaster wanted all the students to meet in the courtyard in the evening. Whose big idea was it to hold a speech outside in January? It was freaking cold. I slipped my coat over my clothes, pulled up the hoodie, and marched to the courtyard with Claire.

It was already dark out, but all the outside lamps had been turned on, giving the night a yellowish glow.

As the students gathered, I noticed the tension in the air was heavy, and many faces were missing. It was like the students had dropped out of the academy after the events from the last semester. Well, if that was true, I couldn't blame them. I for one had thought about not coming back, for two big reasons: I had to search my siblings, and the Shadow Trials. But my mother insisted that this was the safest place for me right now, even with the deadly contest down the road. She said she would do everything in her power to stop it. I didn't know how, if she wasn't allowed on campus anymore.

But Rey was of the same opinion. "If we have to take part in this deadly contest, then so be it. We'll get through it, together."

I liked to think that together we were unstoppable, but we had no idea what the Shadow Trials would consist of. How could he be so sure?

"Hey." A new voice joined us. Harper grinned at us. "Glad to see you two here."

"You too," Claire said with a soft smile.

From what I heard, Claire and Harper had exchanged lots of texts during the long break, though from the looks of it, Claire still had no idea about Harper's feelings.

"How was your break?" I asked, pretending to be ignorant.

"It was okay." Harper shrugged. "You guys know what's going on?"

"That." Claire pointed to the back doors of the Aster building just as they opened and her father walked out.

The staff and professors—including Rey—trailed behind him, forming an arc at his back.

Crimson halted at the bottom of the stairs, and glanced out to the students. "Welcome back to another exciting semester at the prestigious Blackthorn Hunters Academy!" His voice boomed through the courtyard, as if he had swallowed a small microphone.

I scoffed. Exciting semester? What was he saying? That last semester when Randall attacked us, and the one before when Orzon had possessed Tanner, were all *exciting*? He was crazy.

"Besides welcoming you before the first day of classes, I wanted to talk to you about the new rules taking effect at the academy," Crimson went on. "Curfew hours will be changed and enforced. Security on campus has been tightened and the number of guards has increased. Students aren't allowed to leave the academy grounds, except for a couple of scheduled weekends—but with limited hours. The meals will also be scheduled, including snack time," he said, as whispers started across the crowd. So far, the cafeteria had big windows for breakfast, lunch, and dinner, while snacks were always available. But more than just the meals, he was treating us like criminals. All we needed now was a striped jumpsuit and bars on our windows. "Students caught skipping classes will face severe disciplinary action. Guards will be posted at the entrance of every building to make sure everyone is following the rules."

"What about the Shadow Trials?" a half-demon student asked from the middle of the crowd.

"Great question," Crimson said, without losing his fake amusement. "The Shadow Trials will be an extensive contest with multiple phases. As mentioned last semester, not everyone will survive, but those who do will be worthy of attending this academy."

The agitation grew tenfold. People complained and protested, while some said it was all deserved and should be held sooner.

"That's bullshit!" someone shouted from the crowd.

"That kind of language won't be tolerated," Crimson said, as calm as ever. "Now, let me introduce you to two new professors." He gestured to the staff standing behind him. I frowned, confused. I hadn't even noticed there were two new professors. Two men stepped forward. "These are Professor Ivan and Professor Coyne."

"Holy crap," Claire muttered from beside me.

"What?" I asked.

"Those demon hunters," Harper whispered, "are famous."

"Ivan retired a few months ago," Crimson went on. "But I convinced him to come back this semester to teach one of our classes, and to be a judge at the Shadow Trials."

"Professor Ivan," Claire said. "It has a nice ring to it."

I had been studying demon history overtime since I first got to the academy, but I hadn't heard of a famous demon hunter named Ivan. Clearly, I needed to study more modern facts about the demon hunter world.

"How come I've never heard of him?" I asked.

"He was stationed somewhere in Europe," Harper said. Looking at him with pure awe in her eyes, just like Claire.

It wasn't just Claire and Harper who were clearly swooning over Ivan. All the girls and even some of the guys stared at him as if he was some kind of god. I forced myself to look at Professor Ivan too. What was it? Was he handsome? I guess so, with his tall figure, wide shoulders, short black hair, and captivating smile. Maybe it was his charisma?

He addressed the students, greeting them, and some girls swooned.

Okay.

Crimson went on. "Unlike Ivan, Coyne hasn't retired, but I've convinced him to take a break this semester and join us with the same purpose."

I looked around, expecting to see the girls swooning again, but this time, they stared with apprehension.

"What about this one?" I asked my friends.

"He's almost as famous as Ivan, but his personality is said to be hard to deal with," Claire told me. "He argues with fellow demon hunters, and it's said he even killed one once during a fight."

My eyebrows shot up. "On purpose?"

"That's what people say," Harper answered.

Coyne's reception was less warm and more guarded, but even through the apprehension, I could see people were ensnared in his web. I guess being a famous demon hunter, even one with a bad reputation, earned the right to enchant and awe everyone else.

Coyne greeted us with his rough voice and a look of disdain. If he was so unhappy and bothered, why had he accepted the invitation to come here? At least Ivan was kind of handsome and wore a big grin. Coyne was okay with his long legs and slim body, and white-blond hair, but it was the grunts and groans after every move or word that really made him a winner.

Would I have class with them both? I really hoped I didn't.

After the speech, Crimson entered the Aster building with most of the professors and the staff, while the students stayed in the courtyard, complaining about the new rules. The ones with the louder voices were the half-demons, who were discontented about the Shadow Trials.

Well, I was too, as I would have to take part in them. Rey and me.

I noticed when Rey slipped away from the staff and into the crowd. He walked around, as if he was greeting the students, but when he approached the girls and me, he glanced to the side, as if indicating me to follow him.

He entered the Statice building.

"I'll ... meet you back at the dorms," I told Claire and Harper.

The girls chuckled. "Be careful," Harper teased. "You can't be caught."

My cheeks heated up. Like Claire, she knew Rey and I were together, but I still felt a little self-conscious when they teased me like that.

Shaking my head, I joined Rey in the lobby of the Statice building, which was empty since classes wouldn't started until the next day. He saw me coming, grabbed my wrist, and pulled me into the main hallway, away from the glass doors.

"What happened?" I asked, confused.

"With all these rules, it'll be hard for us to see each other," he said, his voice flat. "I don't want you to be caught trying to sneak out to see me."

My brows dipped low. "So you're suggesting we just play professor and student indefinitely?"

He wrapped his hands on my upper arms and pulled me closer. "I don't like this either, Erin, but we both know Crimson is as nuts as Randall. If you're caught, if we're caught, we'll only earn more problems to deal with."

I knew he was right, but that didn't mean I liked it. We had agreed I would sneak into his townhouse a couple of nights per week, and now he was telling me to not do that.

"This sucks," I muttered.

"I know." He slid his hands around my shoulders and embraced me. "But I need to keep you safe."

I rested my chin on his shoulder and rested my hands on his lower back. "You don't need to be my knight in shining armor all the time, you know?"

"Of course I do." Rey pulled back and looked into my eyes. "For example, you'll now go to your dorm, and I'll shift and follow you to make sure you get there safely."

I rolled my eyes. "I hate you."

"No, you don't." He leaned into me, but paused when his lips were an inch from mine. I couldn't help it. I aligned my face with his and rose on tiptoes to close the distance. "See?" he said with a soft chuckle when I pressed my lips on his. "You love me."

I shrugged. "It's true. I do love you."

Serious, he brought a hand up and cupped my face. "And I love you."

He covered my mouth with his and kissed me. I let out a satisfied sigh when he spun us around and pressed me against the wall, his body glued to mine. He ravaged my lips, teased my tongue, and ate me up. A wave of heat coursed through my body as I melted into him, as I felt his hands on my neck, on my back, on my legs. I held on to him for dear life, intent on never breaking this kiss. On never letting him go.

Faint laughter and voices reached our ears, and Rey and I stilled. We waited, my heart thumping hard from our kiss and from the fear of being caught in Rey's arms. Though I hated keeping our relationship a secret, I had to admit it was quite exciting.

Thankfully, the voices went away as fast as they came.

"Some students might have walked by near the doors," Rey said, his voice low. "We better go."

"Right." My shoulders deflated. For the last two plus months we had seen each other almost every day and spent so much time together. It was hard to imagine walking away now, not knowing when I would be able to touch him again.

Holding me tight, Rey rested his forehead on mine. "I promise I'll find a way for us to see each other soon, okay?"

I nodded. "Okay."

He pressed his lips to mine once more before letting me go and stepping back. "Now go. I'll shift and follow."

At first, I couldn't move. I didn't want to. But I knew I had to go. So I forced one foot in front of the other and walked out of the Statice building, through the northwest doors, which led directly to the Gardenia building. I held the doors open for a moment longer, just enough for Rey to fly past them. Then he perched atop the same branch of the same tree from last semester and watched me walk in the women's dorm building.

Feeling defeated, I went directly to my bedroom. I tried distracting myself with normal tasks: taking a shower, getting my stuff ready for tomorrow, and checking if my uniform was clean and pressed.

Later in the night, Claire and Harper stopped by to check on me. We talked a little, they teased me more because of Rey, but my mind and heart weren't in it.

Did they know how much I had suffered, all the things I had gone through, before Rey and I finally got together? Excuse me while I mourned the next few months, when we would have to pretend we didn't love each other.

It was late when they finally left, but even though I stayed in bed and tried closing my eyes, I couldn't fall asleep. I already missed Rey, and I probably missed him this bad because I didn't know when I would see him next. Not as my lover, at least.

An idea popped in my mind. It was crazy and reckless, but almost everything in my life was like that.

I shot up from my bed, changed out of my pajamas and into comfortable jeans and sweater, and took a deep breath, calming myself.

Then, I channeled my magic and teleported out of my bedroom.

4

REY

AFTER MAKING sure Erin was safe in her bedroom, I flew to my townhouse in the Dahlia Villa. It was as big, cold, and empty as I remembered. My heart sank as I imagined Erin coming to spend the night with me, and now with these fucking rules and the increased security, there was no way she could come over.

Unless she got the hang of teleporting.

Fuck, even practicing that would be a problem now.

I tried looking on the bright side. For the first time in my long life, I didn't have any contracts hanging over my head. No deals. Nothing. I was freer than I had ever been. I was here as a professor.

I confess that I was a little fearful when Crimson called me into his office this afternoon. I thought he would try to make another deal, but to my surprise, all the other professors and staff were there too—and then he delivered that speech. Thankfully, Crimson seemed to have lost interest in me.

However, so far freedom didn't taste as great as I expected.

After a shower, I lay down on my bed, wishing it had Erin's scent, like the bed in the loft had, and tried to sleep.

My mind raced as many thoughts raced through my mind.

But one was more prominent: I missed Erin.

Perhaps we should have run away. Better than staying here and apart, and suffering through the Shadow Trials.

But away from the academy, Erin was a beacon for demons. Eventually, King Brikan would find her.

How would I continue searching for Erin's siblings from inside the academy?

Who was Fiona, and where the fuck could we find the witch? It seemed we needed to find even more locator spells since all the ones we had tried so far had failed.

Wait ...

I sat up, trying to focus my thoughts. Sometime ago, I remembered Randall was watching some witches in the area. I didn't know more about it, because he never shared information, but another memory pricked my mind: When I recorded him performing the bloodsbane ritual last semester, he had called the witch by her name.

Were these witches linked? Was Fiona linked to them?

It was a long shot, but right now, I would go after any witch that crossed my path.

Without wasting time, I ran to the guest bedroom, opened the window, shifted into my raven, and flew to the Aster building. While flying, I saw patrols walking down the pathways and stationed at the buildings' entrance. Crimson wasn't really kidding when he said he had increased the campus security.

To enter the Aster building, I had to land on one of the towers and use my magic to open the door. Trudging through the hallways, I had to hide a few times as patrols marched along. So now there were guards inside the buildings?

What was Crimson hiding?

Three doors from Randall's old office, I heard faint footsteps and hid inside one of the meeting rooms. Keeping the lights off, I left a tiny crack in the door and watched while the guard walked by.

Although, it wasn't a guard.

It was Coyne, the famous demon hunter. He was said to have killed another demon hunter on a mission. Rumors ranged from he missed and killed her by mistake to he was enraged and killed her to burn off some of his pent-up frustration.

Why the fuck Crimson had hired such a man to be a professor, or to judge a deadly contest, I would never understand.

As I didn't understand what this man was doing in the corridors of the main building after midnight.

I opened the crack a little more to look at Coyne as he walked away. My suspicion that he was sneaking around was confirmed when he turned a corner and hid behind an archway, seconds before a guard came down the hallway. I hid behind the door, lest the guard see me.

When the guard was done, Coyne continued walking down the hallway, turning his head side to side, as if expecting someone to jump him at any moment.

He went down the stairs.

And I glanced the way he had come. That was where Randall's office was. Had he come from there? Could Crimson still be in his new office and had just talked to Coyne? Or had Coyne sneaked into Crimson's office before me?

After checking if there were more guards coming, I exited my hiding spot and approached the door to Crimson's office. It was not only closed, but locked.

I frowned.

I didn't have time to analyze what Coyne was up to. I used my magic to unlock the door, then slipped in. I conjured a small bolt of darkfire in my hands, and dark light cast a dim glow on the office.

The office was just as Randall had left it. For some reason, I had expected Crimson to burn all the furniture and remodel. Unless he was searching for something.

I sent the darkfire floating in the air and started. I wasn't sure what I was looking for, so I went through everything that caught my eye. The desk drawers and the many documents in them. The shelves beside the desk with books and more documents.

There had to be something somewhere ... something that would mention those witches Randall had been looking for years ago.

Could these documents be in the hidden room at the back of his personal library? I wondered ... had Crimson found that hidden room?

I considered giving up and going there, when I opened the last cabinet and a thick black ledger stared back at me. I picked it up and a jolt coursed through my arms. I almost dropped the fucking thing. Magic protected it. I placed the ledger on top of the desk and directed the darkfire ball to illuminate it. There were scratch marks on the side of the ledger, as if someone had picked up a sharp knife or letter opener and tried to pry it open.

I tsked.

I called my magic and sent it into the ledger. It shook and

sparked. For a moment, I thought it wouldn't open, until finally, it cracked open.

I sat down on the chair and started flipping through the pages. This was a notebook, with random dates, thoughts, lists, and entries. Almost like a diary or planner, where Randall wrote about whatever struck his fancy.

There were entries about Asmodeus, several other princes of the underworld, some higher demons, and even King Brikan. Then, there were entries about Martha, Crimson, other professors. I found a list of herbs used in dark magic, and several spells he was trying to invent.

I also found entries about Erin and me. In my entry, he mentioned how he knew I was a half-demon from the start, but had allowed me to stay anyway. For Erin's entry, he started by saying he had felt a greater destiny within her the moment she stepped into this school. Before he was killed, he had plans to use her and the half-demon army to attack Brikan. He knew about the Demon Kissed Queens too, and if it came to that, he would search for King Brikan's children and use them too.

He also knew about Erin and me, as a couple. He knew about the soul bond and that we had broken it.

Was there anything he hadn't known? I guess that was the only good thing about his immortality and power—he knew and saw everything.

The notes went on and on. About vampires, werewolves, and witches.

The entry was short, but hopeful. He only mentioned he had found the witches he was looking for, and that they were still around. On the same page, he had scribbled the name I was really after: Fiona.

I took pictures of those pages, closed the book, made sure the magic was still in place, and put it back in the cabinet.

Then, I raced out of the office before someone found me.

But as I ran out and later flew back to my townhouse, a sense of purpose filled me. I had found something, a clue. All we had to do now was find these witches, and they would tell us where Fiona was.

5

ERIN

I HONESTLY HAD EXPECTED to teleport a foot inside my room, or smack my nose against the door, or even maybe end up in the middle of the hallway. But when I felt the air whooshing around me stronger than before, the lights shimmering faster than before, I knew I had finally done it.

I had teleported.

But to the wrong damn place.

When I opened my eyes, I nearly crumbled to the floor because I had used too much of my magic, but I stilled myself. I was in a corridor of rough, dark stone.

What the hell? This wasn't Rey's townhouse. For all I knew, this wasn't even inside the academy.

Or was it?

I turned around, recognizing this place. It was the dungeons, where Randall had brought a possessed Tanner and had made Rey and me watch while he exorcised my half-brother.

A scream echoed through the wall and I jumped out of my skin, my heart beating hard against my chest.

What the hell was that? I glanced around. This looked like the dungeons, but the one I had been in had doors lining the walls. This one had none. Just two archways at each end, one leading to another corridor, and the other leading to stairs that climbed upward.

The scream came again and I startled, the hairs on my arms standing on end. The screams were followed by guttural moans and throaty gasps.

One thing I was sure of, it didn't sound human.

With slow steps, I approached the archway that opened to the other corridor. The screams and sounds seemed to be coming from that way. Though I didn't think whoever, or whatever, made the sounds was friendly, my curiosity was bigger than my fear.

Rapid footsteps echoed through the corridor.

Shit.

With my heart in overdrive, I raced to the archway, turned the corner, and pressed myself to the wall, hoping the shadows would cover me. The footsteps grew louder. A moment later, Crimson appeared in the corridors' intersection. I held my breath, sure he was going to see me, but thankfully, he kept marching, turning in the opposite direction instead.

When his footsteps faded, I let out my breath, my hand pressed against my chest.

All right, whatever was down here, this wasn't the time to find out.

I searched the hall, making sure no one was coming, and stepped away from the wall. My first thought was to run up the stairs, back to the Aster building, then out to the Gardenia building, but just to remind me that there were more guards securing the academy, a patrol showed up on the stairs.

Shit. I had no choice here.

Even though I had exhausted most of my magic with the first jump, I had to do it again. I called my magic, coaxing it to fill my veins, to feed my energy.

The air wavered around me, the lights dimmed.

The next thing I knew, I was outside, right beside the Blackthorn tree, in the middle of the courtyard. And there were guards outside the buildings and patrolling the pathways. Before I could think, I teleported again, this time to the lobby of the Gardenia building. If they saw me in that second, they probably thought they were seeing things.

I practically crashed into a decorative vase on the floor.

The guards standing outside the glass doors turned, but I disappeared before they could see me.

I blinked into my bedroom and fell on my bed, breathing hard. Every muscle in my body hurt, and I felt like I couldn't lift a finger even if my life depended on it.

This teleporting thing was fun and useful, in theory, but if I kept making mistakes, it would cost me my life.

Too tired to do anything else, I turned on my side, hugged my pillow, and promptly fell asleep.

My first class of the semester was Defense Against Demons with Professor Ivan. The moment he entered the classroom, all the girls swooned, including Claire.

I frowned. All right, I had already admitted he was handsome, but really? Why were these girls all in love with this older man?

"Good morning," Ivan said, his voice smooth, like

chocolate. "It's a pleasure to come out of my retirement to teach this class to the students of the prestigious Blackthorn Hunters Academy. In this class, we'll learn how to defend ourselves against demons with means other than fighting." His lips pulled up in an easy smile. "It'll be fun, I promise."

Claire rested her elbow on her desk, and her chin on her hand, and practically moaned. "He's amazing."

Well, I couldn't say he was amazing, but I got it. Handsome, nice voice, great smile. He seemed to be a people person.

He started the class by telling us about his last mission before he retired—it had been a raid where he infiltrated one of the underworld lairs and killed hundreds of higher demons, including generals in the princes' legions. He seemed proud of his deed.

"And then, when I thought I was drawing my last breath, a miracle occurred," he said, his tone matching the urgency of the scene. "A burst of energy washed over me, and I felt my stamina increase. I got up, summoned my Dawnblade, and faced the general once again."

Though, I had to admit, he was a good storyteller. He had the entire class ensnared in his story, including me. By the end, we were all holding our breath, wondering how he would make it, and cheering when he told us he had done it. He had cleaned the lair and rid the world of many demons.

"I told you he's amazing," Claire whispered.

"All right, I'll let you have that one," I said in a low voice. "He's pretty cool."

Ruby raised her hand. "Professor Ivan, why did you retire?"

For a second, the professor's contagious smile faded.

"Doesn't everyone know that story? It's a short one. I just got tired."

"That doesn't sound like you," Justin said.

Professor Ivan nodded. "I know. When I thought about it and actually envisioned myself retiring, I was shocked too. But it was time. I'm getting old." He gestured to himself. To be honest, he was good-looking for a man in his fifties. "I didn't want my age and stamina to start taking its toll. I wanted to quit when I was on top."

"Do you regret it, professor?" Claire asked.

"Sometimes," he confessed with a sigh. "I miss the planning, the preparing, the tension, the adrenaline, the rush ... but other than that, I like disappearing from the world, lying on a beach and drinking margaritas all day." Laughter erupted in the classroom. "But I can go back to that next semester. For now, I'll have fun teaching you all, and judging the Shadow Trials."

Carl shot his hand in the air. He was a half-demon. "Professor, what do you think about the Shadow Trials?"

The class went dead silent.

Professor Ivan pressed his lips together, thinking. "I've been invited to the academy to help the students, especially the half-demons, prepare for the Shadow Trials, and to judge the contest. My opinion about it is irrelevant, I'm afraid."

The mood in the classroom became a little somber, except for the few demon hunters students who thought all half-demons were parasites and should be extinct as such.

"Enough of that," Professor Ivan said, his smile returning to his face. "Let's get practicing."

From there, Professor Ivan conducted the class in an open, friendly manner. He told us we would learn quick tricks to deal with demons, like, for example, garrimps liked shiny things. If we found ourselves surrounded by them, we should find anything that could catch their attention, like jewelry, a wristwatch, or broken glass, and throw it far away. They would follow it.

Ha, that was one of the reasons they had attacked me when I was in that haunted house? Because I had been attracted to that necklace—just like them. If I had known this before, I would have thrown it far and run from the house.

Unfortunately, I couldn't change the past.

When the class was dismissed, Claire and I picked up our things and started walking to the door.

"Erin Delman, can I have a minute, please?" Professor Ivan called me.

I froze. Claire looked at me with wide eyes, before pushing me toward him. Other students, mostly females one, glanced at me as if wondering what I had that they didn't.

I turned to the professor. "Yes?"

His eyes followed the rest of the students exiting the classroom. When all of them were out, he brought his gaze to me. "I've heard about what happened last semester."

I gulped. Everyone knew what I had done; why deny it now? "You mean, me using dark magic?"

He leaned into his desk again, practically sitting on its top. "Yes. I also heard that you were almost expelled because of it."

I snorted, then promptly trained my face to a neutral expression. "Sorry. It's just ... I've been almost expelled so many times, I've lost count."

One corner of his lips curled up. "I see. Well, I just wanted to tell you to not let others bully you because of that. Don't be ashamed of the spell you had to use. On the battlefield, we do what we must to survive, and more importantly, to save our friends and family. I know that firsthand."

I stared at him, a little wary of why he was telling me this, but also thankful. It was good to know such a famous demon hunter agreed with my actions, even when I didn't.

Even though I trained to use more dark magic with my mother during the break, I never did it because I liked it. I did it because I came to realize it was necessary. An eye for an eye, wasn't it? King Brikan was the personification of dark magic. If I didn't learn how to use, how to control it, I wouldn't ever stand a chance against him.

"Thank you," I muttered.

"You're welcome." He held my gaze.

Clearing my throat, I took a step back. "I need to go to my next class."

"Of course." Professor Ivan pushed off the desk. "Have a good day, Erin."

"You too, professor," I said, before walking out of his classroom.

As expected, Claire was waiting for me right outside the door. She fell into step with me, practically giggling. I had no doubt she had heard everything he said. She confirmed it once we were on to the stairs.

"He's not only amazing, but caring," she said, her tone dreamy.

Though I was starting to agree with her, I frowned. "Why would such a badass demon hunter be so nice to a half-demon?"

As far as I knew, all demon hunters were brainwashed since birth that all supernaturals were evil, even half-demons. Someone with his reputation and his history, I would have thought he would be the one to throw the first stone at me.

"Because he has a big heart," Claire answered. "But seriously, who cares? At least he seems to be cheering for you. Maybe he'll even give you some great scores during the contest, and you'll win!"

I flinched. Just hearing about the Shadow Trials made me cringe. This damn deadly contest was getting on my nerves. There had to be a way of stopping it, or postponing it.

If I didn't have other problems to worry about now, I would make ruining the Shadow Trials a priority. But for now, I just went with it.

"We'll see," I whispered.

UNLIKE WHAT I EXPECTED, the first day of class went by without any major issues. I had seen some demon hunter students teasing some half-demons students, but despite the urge to go to them and do something, I held it in. There was too much on my plate already. I couldn't risk drawing more attention, or creating a bigger mess.

After our classes of the day were done, Claire and I went to the library. Not that I wanted to, but she insisted we start on one of our assignments.

"The sooner we start, the sooner we'll be rid of it," she said.

I couldn't argue with that.

So, I let her drag me to the library. We picked a table at the back, where there were fewer people, and less noise, and I started making a list of topics for our project while Claire went around, searching for books.

Soon, our table was piled high with plenty of books.

Claire sat down beside me, picked up a book from the pile, and said, "So, what are we researching?"

I glanced at the stack of books. "Are you serious? You brought all of these over, and you haven't decided yet?"

She pointed to my list. "You're still working on the cons and pros of each subject."

No, I wasn't. I was just making a list. No cons and pros. "Why did you grab so many books?"

"Because I thought we could read a little about each topic before deciding," she explained.

So, she wanted to do more work before we did the real work? I knew she liked reading and researching, but this was a little too much for me.

I moved my mouth, but no words came out.

I was saved by Harper, who showed up at our table with a wide grin. "What are you two up to?"

"Researching," Claire announced, sounding very pleased. "Want to join us?"

"Sure," Harper said, though she didn't sound sure at all. She sat on a chair across the table from us and picked up the book closest to her. "What is this about?"

"It's for Demon History." Claire went on, telling Harper about all we had to do for the project. Harper wasn't in our class, though I knew she attended the same course at a different time, so chances were, she would have to work on the same project as us.

However, Harper watched Claire with loving eyes and incredible interest. I was sure more than half of Claire's words were lost to her, but that didn't matter to her. All she wanted was to be able to be close to the girl she liked.

They looked so great together. Damn, how I wanted to help Harper. If only I could make Claire see how much

Harper liked her. I would have to come up with a plan and help Harper; otherwise, they might not get anywhere.

"Hey."

Perking up, I looked over the tall stack of books in front of me and saw as Rey walked to our table.

"Hey," I said back, happy he was here, but a little sad that I couldn't get up from my chair and go to him. When he halted beside our table, I noticed he was way serious. "What's wrong?"

Claire stopped talking and turned to us. Harper blinked, woke up, and glanced at us too.

"I think I found a clue about Fiona," he told me.

"Who's Fiona?" Harper asked.

Right, Claire and Harper didn't know about Tanner's short visit. I quickly told them about it, trying to not say my brother's name, lest Claire remember all she had gone through when he had been possessed by the demon Orzon.

I glanced back to Rey. "What clue?"

"Meet me in the media room in the Gardenia building at midnight," Rey said. "In combat training clothing and a thick coat. I'll explain everything then."

6

REY

RIGHT BEFORE MIDNIGHT, I shifted into my raven and flew from my townhouse to the Gardenia building. As agreed, Erin had left the window of her bedroom open, so I went right in.

Once I flew inside, she shut the window and the curtains.

Then I shifted back into my human form and swept her into my arms.

Erin suppressed a yelp, but she didn't resist. I embraced her tight, buried my face in her hair, and inhaled deeply. "I've missed you."

She knotted her hands around my neck. "It has been just a day, but yeah, I've missed you too."

I brushed her hair aside, turned my head to her neck, and pressed a gentle kiss on the soft spot between her shoulder and neck. Erin's breath caught. I grazed my lips up her throat until her head was back, and she was melting in my arms. I continued the path up, around her chin, and to her mouth. Then I kissed her.

I would have thrown her in bed and shown her how much I had missed her today, but time was short, and we had to get moving.

Reluctantly, I disentangled myself from her. "We should go," I said, though I didn't really mean it. If I had my way, I would spend the entire night in her bed with her.

"Right," Erin said, smoothing down her tee. As I had asked, she wore her combat training clothes—cargo pants, thermal tee, and combat boots. She grabbed her coat and draped it over her arm.

We were careful when opening the door and spying out, but thankfully, there didn't seem to be any patrols inside the dorm building. Perhaps Crimson had been decent enough to keep them outside, to respect the students' privacy.

One could only hope.

When Erin and I entered the media room, Claire and Harper were already there, waiting in the dark.

I closed the door, conjured a small darkfire as light, and told them to sit down. I took a spot next to Erin and began, "I found notes from Randall saying he knew about some witches hiding nearby. I'm guessing they have a small coven."

"All right," Claire said, "I'm not following."

"Fiona's name was scribbled in those notes," I told them.

The girls' eyes bugged.

"So, if we find these witches, we find Fiona?" Erin asked, her voice filled with hope.

"I'm not sure, as the notes didn't really explain anything, but I'm guessing they at least know who she is," I said. "Maybe where to find her."

"And where is this coven?" Harper asked.

"There were vague directions in Randall's notes, but I

think I know where it is," I said. "Now, my plan is to go there right now. Hence why I asked you to wear your combat uniform. And a coat, because it's going to be cold." I gestured to their clothing. "But I understand if you guys don't want to come."

Erin narrowed her eyes in a you're-kidding-right kind of look.

"I'm in," Claire said. "My only question is how we're going to evade all the demon hunter guards around the campus."

"Simple." I stood up. The girls mimicked me. Then I took Erin's hand. "Erin will teleport us out of here."

Her eyes became two huge circles. "What? I can't do it! Especially not carrying all of you with me."

I squeezed her hand. "I'll lend you my power and focus. With our magics linked, you'll be able to do it, I'm sure." She hesitated for a moment, but then nodded. I glanced at Claire and Harper. "Are you two in?"

Claire grunted. "Ugh, I didn't even know you could teleport." But she slipped her hand into Erin's.

"Sorry, it's a new thing," Erin said. "I just forgot to tell you."

"If you promise not to teleport us into the middle of a wall, I'm in." Harper took Claire's hand and mine, closing the circle.

"Erin, just focus on taking us outside the walls," I told her. "I'll do the rest."

She dipped her chin once and closed her eyes. I called my magic and sent it to her. She didn't resist it, and my magic blended with hers as if they had been cut from the same cloth. As if they belonged together. As if we still had the soul bond and still had our souls linked.

Once more the truth smacked me in the face: Erin was my soulmate, and she would always be. I didn't need a fucking soul bond to tell me that.

Erin took in a deep breath, absorbing my magic, shaping it to her will. Around us, the air wavered, the lights shifted, and the world revolved. For a brief moment, it was like we were floating in a dark cloud.

Then, our feet landed on something hard and the world stabilized.

"You did it," I said, looking around. Even though it was pretty dark here, I could clearly see we were a hundred feet or so away from the academy's outer wall, right at the edge of the forest, our feet sank half a foot into the snow. I stared at Erin, in awe. "You did it."

She smiled at me. "Only because you helped."

Claire and Harper dropped our hands, but I only held on to Erin's tighter. "But now you know how it is, how it feels. I bet you can do it by yourself now." Why hadn't I thought of that earlier? She would probably be a pro at teleporting by now if we had started that way.

Claire glanced to the dark forest. "What now?"

"Now, we keep teleporting in small jumps, until we arrive at the location I saw in the notebook," I said.

Erin frowned. "How will I know where to take us?"

"I'll guide you somehow," I told her. I hoped this fucking worked. "Ready?"

We joined our hands again. Erin closed her eyes and summoned her magic. Thinking about the place we had to go, I sent my magic into Erin.

It took several jumps, but we were finally close. Afraid of startling the witches, we went up the mountain slowly.

Claire shivered. "You could have told us where we were

coming. Then I would have brought snow boots, mittens, and a wool hat."

"Me too," Harper said.

"Sorry, I didn't think that far ahead," I said. "I was just eager to get here and find out more."

"Well, in Rey's defense, he did tell us to bring a coat," Erin added.

I glanced at her. Only she would side with me right now. At least here the trees were so close together, their leafless branches entwining, that the snow was a thin cover on the ground.

"We should be close," I said, hurrying my steps. We passed a few trees, then they were gone, giving away to a large clearing with a building in the center. "Wait." I raised my hand, signalizing the girls to stop.

They halted by my side and stared out.

"This doesn't look like a witch coven," Erin muttered.

A heavy breath escaped my lips. "No, it doesn't."

It was a fucking prison. The building in the center was a square box with no windows. Demon hunter guards stood by the main doors, and more walked around the perimeter.

Two of them rounded a corner, coming closer to us. The girls and I retreated deeper into the trees and crouched down, spying on them.

"What are you thinking?" Erin asked.

"The witches must be locked inside," I said.

Claire frowned. "How do you know? Maybe there are no witches inside."

"But they are guarding something," Harper said. "Otherwise, why this secrecy? Why the hiding? Why so many guards?"

I nodded. "I still think the witches are in there." That was what I had concluded from Randall's random notes.

"So, what now?" Claire asked.

"We need to ask them about Fiona." Erin shrugged. "Maybe she's in there with them."

"You mean, we're freeing them?" Harper asked.

I nodded. "I think so. We knock out the guards, and free them."

"What if they are evil?" Claire asked.

I got that she was always careful and liked to research and analyze all details before acting, but it was starting to get on my fucking nerves. We didn't have time to overthink this right now.

"We'll deal with them, then," I said.

Erin nodded at me. "Let's do this."

I was glad she took the initiative and stood up as the guards walked past our spot. They startled, probably not expecting anyone, but before they could react, Erin enveloped them in darkfire, creating a small, black tornado around them. Three seconds later, their bodies hit the ground, softened by the snow.

She glanced at us. "It won't take them long to wake up."

Then she dashed into the clearing.

With a proud smile, I followed her.

But she was too quick. Erin conjured her zombies and sent them to attack the demon hunters. Because of the ruckus, all the guards came to fight the zombies. From there, it was easy to sneak up on them and put them to sleep, either with an arm lock, a punch, or magic.

The door wasn't a big hassle. We got the magical keys from one of the guards and simply unlocked it.

Then, we stepped inside the building.

Erin conjured darkfire and sent it to the ceiling, where it illuminated the room.

At least two dozen witches sat around a mostly empty room, ranging from four, maybe five years old, to fifty. My stomach sank as I noticed they looked dirty and malnourished.

The oldest stood up and came forward, confronting us. "You're not taking any witches today."

Erin raised her palms, in a peace gesture. "We aren't here to hurt you. We're here to help you escape."

The old woman's shoulders sagged. "W-what?"

"Come with us," I told them. "We'll take you to safety."

"We should hurry," Claire said. "The guards won't stay down forever."

The oldest witch ushered the others to move. It took them a minute, but once they were all up and out, their strength made an appearance.

But I noticed they were underdressed for the weather, so I grabbed a coat from one of the unconscious guards. They could hide from the cold in the building when they woke up. Noticing what I was doing, Erin, Claire, and Harper started stripping the fallen guards. We passed the jackets along, though there wasn't enough for all of them.

"Let's go!" I shouted, taking the front. The four of us separated. While I took the lead, Erin took the back, and Claire and Harper flanked the witches.

"Where are you taking us?" the oldest witch asked, sounding apprehensive. I was sure that having the four of us spread out like that seemed rather suspicious, but it was only for their safety. We didn't want any of them to fall behind.

"First, we get away from here," I told her. "After that, we'll decide."

To make sure we couldn't be easily followed, Erin dropped branches over our footsteps, sometimes she smoothed the snow with more branches, and whenever we could, we crossed over small rocks and stones, to not leave any trail behind.

Though I didn't think they had enough energy for that, we marched down the mountain for almost two hours, to make sure we would be safe from the guards for at least a little while. Then, we stopped in a small area where the snow was sparse and the trees were thick.

The older witch told the others to sit down and rest, then she came to me.

"What is going on?" she asked. "Why did you rescue us?"

Erin came to stand by my side, while Claire and Harper tended to the witches. "We'll get to that, but first ... let me assure you, all of you are safe now. I'm Erin. This is Rey. That one is Claire, and that is Harper," she said, pointing to the girls. "What is your name?"

The old witch hesitated. "I'm Joan."

I saw the disappointment in Erin. This wasn't the one she was looking for.

"Nice to meet you, Joan," Erin said. Her calm and gentleness surprised me sometimes. "Tell us, why were you locked up there?"

Joan crossed her arms. "That evil demon hunter ... Randall is his name. He kidnapped all of us and locked us in there."

I sucked in a sharp inhaled. "Let me guess. Once a month, he came and took one of you away. The last one was named Brielle."

Her eyes widened. "How do you know that?"

"Because I saw what he did to her."

Joan put her hand over her mouth. "No. Don't tell me. I don't want to know. He takes them away and they never return. I always hoped they would either escape, or that we were mistaken and he was actually taking care of them."

"I'm sorry," Erin whispered.

The witch nodded. "He hasn't come in a long while, though. I'm thankful for that, but still, it sets all of us on edge."

"Randall is dead," I told her.

Her jaw fell to the ground. "W-what?"

I was guessing that, with Randall dead, no one came to take the witches, and without a direct command from their boss, the guards kept them locked there, waiting.

"You're free now," Erin told her. "You can go back to your covens."

Joan's lips curled down. "That's ... good news, but most of us have been gone for so long, and some of us never had a coven." She eyed the little girls in group. This was fucking painful. "I'm not sure we have anywhere to go now."

"We'll work on that," Erin said, her voice gentle.

Tired of waiting, I asked, "Tell me, are any of the witches named Fiona in your group?"

Joan shook her head. "No."

"Have you meet or heard of a witch named Fiona?" I insisted.

"No," Joan repeated. "If you're after a witch, I think your best bet is to contact the witch queen of the Silverblood coven. A girl from her coven was kidnapped last year, and killed recently. She told us about how the witch queen was different from the rest, that she and her husband plan to change the supernatural world."

Silverblood coven? I knew this ... "You mean Queen Thea?"

"Yes, that's her name," Joan confirmed. "It's said her daughter is the next Queen of All Witches, which means she'll rule over all witches, regardless of coven."

"So, if we contact Thea, she can take care of all of you," Erin said, musing.

Joan shrugged. "I would like to believe so."

From there, we hatched a plan and executed it. We took the group of witches farther down the mountain, until we arrived at a small village bordering the mountain. There, I went to an ATM machine and took out some cash. Then I took Joan to the only inn in the town, where she spelled the attendant to give her several rooms, afraid he would find it suspicious there were two dozen women coming to crash in the middle of the night. Even so, I paid for the rooms and gave the witches the rest of the money. Since I thought they were hungry, I told them to buy snacks from the vending machines for now. Tomorrow morning, they should buy food, and possibly some jackets too. I told them to lie low, to not go out all at the same time, and to keep checking the clerk working at the inn's desk. If the clerk changed, they had to spell that person too.

Meanwhile, I would return to the academy and contact Thea. Hopefully, the witch queen would do something about these witches. Otherwise, I didn't know.

The girls and I bid them goodbye.

On the way back to the forest, Erin slipped her hand in mine. "We did good, right? Freeing them?"

I nodded. "I think so. From what I heard, Queen Thea is a good witch. She'll know what to do." At least, I hoped she would. "Moreover, if someone knows about Fiona, it'll be her."

Erin nodded. "One can only hope."

Tired and fucking cold, the girls and I trudged through the forest, toward the academy. This had been just our first day back at the academy. It kind of made me dread the rest of the semester.

7

ERIN

"How are they?" I asked Rey as he grabbed the ice cream from the fridge. He had gone to visit the witches this afternoon, to check on them, while I was in class. It had been almost a week since we rescued them. I was starting to get anxious, because even though they had magic, it would be impossible to hide two dozen witches in a small town for much longer.

That night, we had gotten back to the academy at sunrise. After dropping us off at the Gardenia building, Rey shifted into his raven and flew to his house, where he would find a way to contact Queen Thea.

In the end, he called a werewolf alpha named Luana, who apparently he had met because of Wyatt, the werewolf who had helped us when I first came to the academy. Luana was close to Thea, and after explaining what was happening, Rey called Thea. She said she was grateful that he reached out to her, but it would take her a few days to come to Colorado. Rey assured her he would check on the witches every couple of days to make sure they were all right.

"They are fine," Rey answered, grabbing two spoons from the utensils drawer. "Agitated, eager to leave, but fine. Not hungry, or cold, or dirty anymore, at least." He sat down on the stool next to me and put the ice cream tub on the island in front of us. "I told them Thea is supposed to come tomorrow night, and they looked relieved."

I dug into the ice cream. "I bet they are."

I couldn't imagine what they had gone through. Being kidnapped by Randall, kept in that room for years, underfed, maltreated, worse than animals ready for the slaughter. And some of them were little kids, without their mothers, just suffering in silence. That had to be traumatizing.

I couldn't think of that without feeling sick to my stomach.

Which reminded me of another scene that had made me sick, but with all that had happened since then, I had forgotten to tell Rey about it.

"Hm, you know, on our first day here, I tried teleporting to your townhouse."

He turned his gray eyes to me. "What the fuck? You didn't come here. What happened?"

I played with my spoon. "I ended up in some kind of dungeon, like the one we went to with Randall when he exorcised Tanner, but it was different somehow. Maybe some other side of the dungeons?"

Rey's body went rigid. "That's ... that's fucking dangerous, Erin."

"I know, don't grill me about it just yet," I said. "I wanted to tell you this because I heard screams when I was down there. Desperate screams and moans. I saw Crimson too."

"What?" Rey almost shrieked. "Your story is getting worse by the minute."

"Don't worry, he didn't see me. I'm just worried about what he's up to down there. We were so shocked when we found out Randall was making sacrifices for powers. What if Crimson is doing the same? And right here, inside the academy."

He shook his head, his messy hair falling over his eyes. "Erin ... I get it, you want to help, as always. That's a noble trait, but please, don't go poking around dungeons like that. You can end up trapped. You get that, right?"

"I do, but—"

"I promise you this, when all our own problems are solved, we can look into that, all right?" he said, his eyes pleading. "Just don't go wandering alone and finding new trouble for us, okay?"

I snorted. Yeah, because I was quite the troublemaker.

But still, the thought of witches, humans, or even demons locked in the dungeons didn't sit well with me. That, plus the poor witches we rescued made me too worried to stay quiet and relaxed.

So I did my best to forget about it for a while, which wasn't hard when Rey was by my side, wearing nothing more than black sweatpants. I shoved another spoonful of ice cream in my mouth and glanced at him, at how the muscles of his arms and shoulders flexed and popped as he moved his arm and ate his ice cream.

If we hadn't just left his bed, I would be all over him.

Well, maybe, that wasn't such a bad idea.

I licked my spoon.

Rey arched an eyebrow at me. "What is going on inside that pretty head?"

I turned toward him, reached up with my legs, scooted closer, hopped on his lap, and wrapped my legs around his waist. "This," I told him. "This scene was happening in my mind." I dropped my spoon and cupped his face. I brushed my lips over his and he let out a groan.

"That's not fair," he whispered against my mouth. He rose from the stool, taking me with him, and deposited me on the island. "Now, this is better." He leaned into me, capturing my mouth and deepening the kiss.

Holy shit, if we kept that up, I wouldn't go back to my dorm room tonight, which would be bad, really bad.

The last time we had spent the entire night together was over a week ago, when we were still living in West Hill. About four days ago, Rey had snuck into my room through the window in the middle of night, but since the walls were thin there, we hadn't done more than hold each other and sleep.

So, even though he had said it was risky, he had seemed happy when I teleported to his townhouse just after midnight. We had fooled around in his bed for a couple of hours, broken up for a night snack, and now it seemed we would go for it again.

At this rate, I better become a night owl.

Sleep was overrated, wasn't it?

***

THE SUN WAS RISING when I finally teleported back to my dorm room.

Since I didn't have classes first period, I went back to bed and slept for a couple of hours before getting up, taking a shower, putting on my uniform, and heading to class.

I stepped out of the Gardenia building, took three steps out, and found Tom marching down the path, coming straight at me. Really, this again? He had murder written all over his face, and I knew this would only get worse when he summoned his Dawnblade.

Hands raised high, I retreated a few steps. "Tom, stop." I really wished he would listen to me. This time, I wouldn't let him hurt me. I wouldn't let him touch one strand of my hair. "I'm warning you, stay back."

But he didn't listen to me. In broad daylight—as a few students walked by us, and then stopped to gawk, but didn't do anything to help—Tom raised his sword and lunged at me. I quickly raised a wall of darkfire and retreated.

Tom's sword hit the wall and bounced back, his arm shaking with the force of the impact. "Come here, you little bitch!"

He ran around the shield, his sword ready to strike through my head again.

I called my magic, intent on summoning the darkfire and having it wrap around him so he couldn't move, when Professor Ivan ran out of the Statice building.

"Tom Heyward, stop!" Professor Ivan summoned his Dawnblade and parried Tom's strike. Like a dancer, he spun around and then elbowed Tom hard on the ribs, making him loose his grip around his sword, then the professor brought his arm up, jarring Tom's hand. The sword fell, but before it reached the ground, Professor Ivan spun again, crouched a little, and picked up the sword by the hilt.

Holy shit, he was good.

The swords disappeared, and Professor Ivan held Tom's arms, pulling them behind his back. "Care to explain yourself, Tom?"

Tom shot me a glare and spat at the ground right in front of my feet. "This mongrel is infecting our school. She needs to die. All of them need to die."

Professor Ivan pulled Tom's hands harder. "Saying those nasty things aren't helping your case."

Movement caught my eyes, and I saw Professor Coyne watching everything from the entrance of the Statice building, a half-grin on his lips.

Crimson rounded the corner of the building, walking toward us as if he was strolling through a park. A second later, Rey appeared from behind him, running toward me.

At the last second, he remembered his position and halted a safe three feet from me. "Are you okay?" he asked, his voice holding a slight tremor, and his eyes turning silver with worry and anger.

I nodded. "I am. Professor Ivan showed up just in time." I gestured to him. "Thank you," I said. I was grateful the professor came out when he did; otherwise, I would have hurt Tom, and right now, he would look like the victim, not me.

"Don't mention it," the professor said, still holding tight to a jerking Tom.

"What's going on here?" Crimson asked, just now getting to us.

"Tom Heyward attacked Erin Delman," Professor Ivan said. "I intercepted the attack before it turned into something worse."

Halted between us, Crimson glanced from me to Tom, his lips turned upside down, as if being here bored him to death. "Tom, I'll let you go with a warning: do not attack the students anymore, even if they are half-demon." He practically spat the last two words. When Professor Ivan didn't let go of Tom, Crimson stared at him. "I said he can go."

"But he attacked another student," Professor Ivan protested, his voice going up a tiny bit. From the hard set of his jaw, it was easy to see he was holding back. "He needs to have a disciplinary action, at least."

"I said let him go," Crimson repeated, his tone harsher, pointed. With an exasperated sigh, Professor Ivan dropped Tom's arms. The guy had the audacity to glare at me before stomping away. "As for you," Crimson started, turning to me. "Let this serve as a warning. Do not provoke other students if you don't want to get in trouble."

My jaw hit the floor. "What the—?"

"Erin didn't do anything," Rey said, cutting off the curse and ugly words I would have spewed at our headmaster. "She just defended herself."

"Did she?" Crimson asked. "We'll never know. For now, resume your normal schedule."

With that, he walked away.

Staring at his back, I clenched my fists. "That was ..." I pressed my lips tight before I regretted the words that sprouted on my tongue. I let out a long breath and faced Professor Ivan. "Thank you," I repeated. "I didn't plan on hurting him, but if you hadn't showed up, I would have done something to defend myself, and clearly, we can see I would have been in trouble for that."

Professor Ivan nodded. "I'm just upset the headmaster dismissed Tom. If it were me, I would have sent him to detention." He glanced at Rey, then back at me. "Anyway, I was about to start class before I came out." He pointed to the Statice building. "Excuse me."

"Sure," I mumbled as he walked away from us.

When he disappeared inside the building and the crowd thinned as the students went to their classes, Rey took a step closer to me. "Are you sure you're all right?"

I nodded. "Yup."

Rey let out a long breath. "It seems I can't leave you alone for a minute. Not even during the day."

"It's okay, Rey, relax." I started raising my arms, to touch him, but controlled myself and put my arms down. "I wasn't going to let him beat me up this time. If I had to, I would even strike and hurt him, but he wasn't going to win this time."

One corner of Rey's lips curled up. "Good girl. Sadly, that doesn't ease my concerns." He glanced at his wristwatch. "You're late for class. How about skipping it completely and spending the next hour with me?"

I faked a gasp. "What? A professor suggesting I skip classes?"

"I'm saying it as a worried boyfriend, not a professor."

"Hm, so you're my boyfriend," I whispered, feeling all warm inside.

He cocked an eyebrow. "Am I not?"

"All right, boyfriend." I smiled at him. "I like that idea."

"Go back to your dorm." He jerked his chin to the building behind me. "I'll watch until you're inside. Then, I'll shift into my raven and fly to your window."

I nodded, then practically skipped into the Gardenia building. In the end, this almost getting beat up thing was giving me an extra hour with Rey.

I liked it.

I STAYED with Erin for a little over an hour, then we both had to go to our respective classes. But I checked on her all the fucking time, even between my classes when I had only ten minutes. I looked like a creeper again, but I felt that was better than having her delivered to me all wounded like last semester.

In the end, the day went by fast.

Around ten at night, I went back to Erin's room to check on her, and after putting her to sleep, I flew out of the window and went to the town, since it was almost time to meet with the witch queen of the Silverblood coven.

We agreed to meet outside of town, where no one would see us, and when I got there at exactly midnight, Thea was already there. She was more beautiful than I imagined, with long blond hair, bright gray eyes, and a posture to make any ballerina envious.

She wasn't alone, though.

She introduced me to Drake, the lord of DuMoir castle, and her mate. Like her, he was good-looking with black hair and green eyes. If I didn't know he was a powerful vampire lord, I would have guessed from his stance.

With them were two others: a witch called Elisa, and a vampire named Cain—their right hands.

"Thank you for contacting me," Thea said, her voice gentle. "I'm eager to meet the witches you mentioned."

"This way." I gestured downhill, where the forest opened and the inn appeared in the distance. Once we got close, I stopped and said, "Wait here."

I went alone to retrieve the witches. Joan was ready, and once I told her it was time, she sent out the first group of witches. Because they were too many and we didn't want to have to spell anyone else, the witches left the inn in small groups, until all of them had evacuated the rooms.

When Joan and I got back to the group in the shadows, the witches stood hunched together, all watching Thea, Drake, and their companions with huge eyes.

"It's okay," Thea said, her voice even kinder than before. She took a step forward. "We're your friends, and we're here to help you."

"It's okay, girls," Joan said. "Queen Thea is telling the truth."

The witches visibly relaxed a little and Thea threw Joan a smile.

Drake approached me. "You said you're from the Blackthorn Hunters Academy, right?"

I nodded. "That's correct."

He narrowed his eyes. "I thought demon hunters killed all supernaturals on sight."

"Unlike most demon hunters, I know not all supernaturals are evil," I explained.

"If only all demon hunters were like you, our world would

be much better off," Drake mused. "Perhaps if there was an academy like that where all supernaturals could co-exist ..."

I frowned. For the first time, I wondered what would happen to the demon hunter society if they ever learned the truth, that not all supernaturals were evil. Would it crumble? Would it rebel? Would it cause a civil war? The thought put me on edge.

Thea had Elisa and Cain guide the witches away. Before going with them, Joan dipped her head to me. I waved at her.

Drake bid me goodbye and followed them, but Thea came back.

"I just wanted to thank you again," she said, sounding pleased. "If there's ever anything I can do for you, don't hesitate to call me."

"Actually," I started, "there's something I want to know. I'm looking for a witch named Fiona."

Thea lost her smile and her brows pinched. "Why are you looking for her?"

I considered it for a minute. Should I tell her? "I'm studying a prophecy, and I think she was the one who made it. I would like to talk to her about it."

"To be honest, I haven't seen her in years," Thea said. "She isn't a Silverblood witch, so my contact with her was already limited to begin with."

"So you don't know where to find her," I said, disappointed.

"No, I don't, but the last I heard, she had moved to the middle of the country." She paused for a moment. "Or was it central west? Well, I don't know. She might have moved again."

I nodded. "It's okay."

"When I get back to the Silverblood coven, I'll ask my witches about Fiona. If I learn anything new, I'll let you know."

"That would be great. Thanks."

She nodded. "Thank you again for saving these witches. Take care, Rey." She spun around and followed her mate and their companions.

To my surprise, the other vampire walked past her and came to me.

"Can I help you?" I asked, a little wary about this vampire coming to me when everyone else was already gone.

Cain halted about five feet from me. "I wanted to ask you ... do you know Norah?"

I frowned. "You mean, the demon hunter, Norah? Blond hair, green eyes?"

Cain nodded. "That would be the one."

"I know her, yes, but I haven't seen her in three, maybe four months," I said, confused. Why was he asking about Norah?

"Is she all right?"

"Yes, last I saw her was right after a battle, but she was okay."

Cain let out what sounded like a relieved breath. "Good. That's all I wanted to know. Thanks."

The vampire zoomed away with his super speed, catching up with the others in a second.

And I stood there, a little lost about the last two minutes. Cain knew Norah? He was interested in her well-being? I had always thought it had been strange how Norah had helped that day with Farrah, and later defended Erin when the school board wanted to expel her for being a half-demon. I clearly remembered her words when I asked why she was helping us.

"I have my reasons," she had said.

Could Cain be that reason? If so, they were star-crossed lovers. Erin would love this bit of gossip.

9

AVA STEPPED AWAY from my kick, then advanced on me, her fist coming for my jaw. I went down in a deep horse stance and landed an elbow strike on her stomach.

Grunting, she stumbled back. "If I weren't wearing this shitty chest guard," she mumbled, obviously wanting to rough me up too. She inhaled deeply and started coughing. "Let's take a break." Ripping the chest guard off, Ava sat down on the mat.

I glanced at Professor Genevieve. She was helping other students. She had seen us before and even complimented us. I guessed she would be okay if we took a short break.

I loosened my chest guard and sat beside Ava. "Sorry if I hit you too hard," I said as I watched the other students during our martial arts class.

Ava shrugged. "We're supposed to hit hard." She glanced at me, her expression guarded. "I heard about Tom trying to corner you again yesterday. I'm sorry about that."

"It's not your fault."

"I know, but he still carries the same last name as I do,"

she said, her voice unusually low. "You know, he has been acting weird. Our family got together during winter break, which was terrible by the way, and he was an even bigger jerk than usual. Everyone in my family complained, even his parents, who usually defend him no matter what."

"I really don't care that much about Tom," I told her. "As long as he doesn't bother me, I don't care at all." I glanced at Ava and found she was focused on something on the other side of the classroom.

Not something. Someone.

Harvey sparred with Justin, but he didn't seem into it. Before, his sparring partner had been Peter, one of his closest friends. A pang cut through my heart. Peter had died last semester when Tornar, then Randall attacked the school. For some reason, it all felt like my fault.

"He has been really sad about Peter," Ava whispered.

I frowned. She had also lost a friend last semester. "What about you? Aren't you sad about Ruby?"

She turned her blue eyes to me. "I am. I'm sad and upset that we hadn't been in a good place when she died. I wished I could go back in time and at least give her a proper goodbye."

For the last year or so, Ava had been distancing herself from her two best friends, Stella and Ruby. There were moments when they all argued and fought and spent weeks without talking to each other. They were in one of these phases when Ruby died.

"I'm sorry," I whispered.

Ava inhaled deeply. "One thing my father always told me was to not get too attached to anyone, not even to the man I love, because our occupation brings so much loss. You won't hurt if you're not attached to anyone."

I shook my head. "I think it's the opposite. Because being

a demon hunter is so dangerous, we have to get attached even more. We can't hold back. We can't wait until tomorrow to show our feelings, to have a good day, to say I'm sorry, and make more friends." I nudged her with my elbow. "What are you waiting for?"

She cut me a glare. "You mean Harvey?"

"Who else?"

"Where were you when we pranked him last semester? He practically humiliated me that night." Her gaze returned to him. "I should give up. That way I won't suffer anymore." Startling me, Ava shot up. She picked up her chest guard. "Come on. We can go a few more rounds before the end of class."

Frowning, I pushed to my feet and tied the chest guard around myself again. If someone asked me, I would say Ava was hiding from her own feelings. She clearly loved Harvey. She had loved him for a long time now. Why pretend as if she didn't?

I glanced at Harvey, making a mental note to talk to him about Ava.

I rolled my shoulders and faced Ava as she lunged at me.

AFTER ALL MY classes were done for the day, I dragged my tired feet back to the dorm building. A few feet above my head, a certain raven flew by, checking on me. A faint smile curved my lips. Rey had told me he felt both like a creeper and my protector for checking on me so many times a day. I told him I didn't care, as long as he actually came to me at some point, because just looking at his raven all day didn't really put me at ease.

I climbed up the stairs, imagining how my night would be. I was so damn tired, but I still wanted him to come and stay with me for a couple of hours, even if it was just to hold me until I slept again.

"Erin!"

I heard my name and turned. Harper jogged toward me. "Hey, my grandmother called this morning. She said you still didn't return her wand and spell book."

I gasped. "I didn't?" I raced to my bedroom, and checked under the bed, where I had hidden the items after Rey and I broke the soul bond. "Holy shit," I muttered as I pulled the spell books and the black box. "I don't know what to say. I ... I wasn't in my right mind and—"

"Don't worry,' Harper said with a small smile. "She said you were probably so affected with the breaking of the soul bond, that you forgot everything else." She pointed to the items. "But she really would like them back now."

"Of course." I picked up the book and wand box and offered them to Harper. "Here."

"No, you're helping me."

"What? How?"

Harper showed me a sheet of paper with the official academy seal. "I've got permission for the three of us—you, Claire, and me—to go out this evening and meet my grandmother."

I stared at her. "How?"

She shrugged. "I honestly don't know. I was sure I would be denied. But here it is. Are you ready to go?"

I glanced around. Was I ready? I had no homework, no training, it was too early for dinner, and even early to meet Rey.

Rey.

He would be pissed if I left without warning him.

"Give me a moment," I said, reaching for my phone. I sat down on my bed and texted him.

Me: *Hey. Harper, Claire, and I are going to Chasseur Ville. I need to return the wand and spell book to Harper's grandmother.*

A minute passed, then there was a ding:

Rey: *Right now? I can't go right now.*

Me: *It's okay, you don't need to come.*

Rey: *It'll be dangerous.*

Me: *In a town full of demon hunters?*

Rey: *The demon hunters might attack you.*

Me: *Rey ...*

Rey: *Okay. Fine. But I'll at least fly with you until you leave the academy.*

Me: *Fine by me.*

Rey: *And you have to text me every 5 minutes.*

Me: *Aren't you a little too much?*

Rey: *Fine. 10 minutes.*

Me: *I'll text you when I get there, and when I'm back in the academy. Then, you can come put me to bed.*

Rey: *Deal.*

Me: *See you later.*

Rey: *Be safe.*

I jumped from my bed and faced Harper. "Let's go."

ON PURPOSE, I sat in the back of Claire's car, so Harper would seat in the front with Claire. I lowered my head, pretending to text Rey, letting them to talk by themselves.

Unfortunately, they didn't say much the entire drive.

When we got there, Francine was waiting for us at her

porch, and when we entered her house, I smelled the honey cookies right away.

I handed her the spell book and wand. "I'm so, so sorry I forgot about these."

"It's okay, my dear," Francine said as she beckoned us to sit in the living room with her.

"You were right," I said as we followed her in. "Rey and I shouldn't have broken the soul bond. It was a mistake."

She glanced at me over her shoulder. "You can choose your heart's path regardless of any bond." She put the spell book and the wand on the shelf and turned back to us. "Isn't that right?"

My cheeks heated up. Did she know Rey and I were together? How?

Standing by my side, Harper said, "Yum!"

As I thought, she had a plateful of honey cookies waiting for us. "Please, help yourselves," Francine said, as she sat down in an armchair.

The girls and I sat down on the couch and dug in. In less than a minute, we had devoured half of the cookies. Dinner what? This was dinner and dessert.

"These are amazing," I mumbled, my mouth full.

Francine smiled. "Glad they please you." The wise woman narrowed her eyes at me. "I can sense some other dilemma troubling you now. Tell me about it."

I stared at her. How did she know these things? Wait, Francine was a witch. Maybe she knew about Fiona. "I'm looking for a witch. Her name is Fiona, and I was told she's the one who made the Demon Kissed Queen prophecy." Francine's brow furrowed as her gaze lowered to my hands. Did she know about this prophecy too? I rolled up the sleeve of my jacket and showed her the mark on my wrist. "Supposedly, this prophecy is about me and two other girls."

"I see," she said, her voice calm.

"Grandma, do you know about this prophecy?" Harper asked.

"I've heard about it," Francine said.

My eyes bugged. "You know the entire prophecy? Could you tell me?"

Francine shook her heard. "It was many years ago. I didn't pay attention to it back then." She glanced at my wrist again. "That's why you want to speak with Fiona? To hear the prophecy in its entirety?"

"Well, yes, but also, since she was the one who foresaw it, maybe she can help me find the other two women depicted in the prophecy."

"We've tried several tracking spells, but none worked," Claire added.

Francine rose from her seat, went to the same shelf where her spell book and wand were stored, and grabbed two items. She came back to the armchair and spread out what looked like an old yellow map on the coffee table, and then placed a small crystal over it.

"If you imbue the crystal with your magic, and let a drop of your blood fall on this map, it should do the trick," Francine said.

"What?" I stared at the items in front of me. "That simple?"

"Well, this is a special map and a powerful crystal," she said. "Combined with your magic and your blood, it should work."

I grabbed the crystal in my hand and instantly felt the

magic inside it, pulsing against my palm. "I can feel it." I glanced at Francine. "How do I do it?"

"It's simple," Francine said. "Prick your finger and let a drop of your blood fall in the center of the map. It'll disappear—don't worry about that. Hold the crystal above the map, like this." She guided my arm to the right position. "And think about who you want to find."

"Don't I need something of theirs?" At least, all the dozens of spells Claire had found needed an item from the person we were trying to find.

Francine smiled at me. "Your blood is acting as a magical agent in this spell, and also as the link to your siblings."

I gasped. Why had I never thought of that? "Wow, I'm so stupid."

"You're far from stupid." She folded the map and handed it to me. "Here, take them and do this spell on a quiet day, when you're relaxed. It'll work the best then."

I took the folded map from her. "Thank you." If I had my way, I would be doing the spell right now, but we already had imposed too long. Francine would never know how grateful I was for all she had done for me. "I promise I'll remember to return these to you when I'm done with them."

She chuckled. "That's fine, my dear. As long as you accomplish what you want, it's all fine."

After a few more cookies and small talk, Francine saw us to the front door. We went back to the academy, with me holding the map and the crystal tight. A renewed sense of confidence and purpose filled me, and I felt ready for the challenges ahead.

10

REY

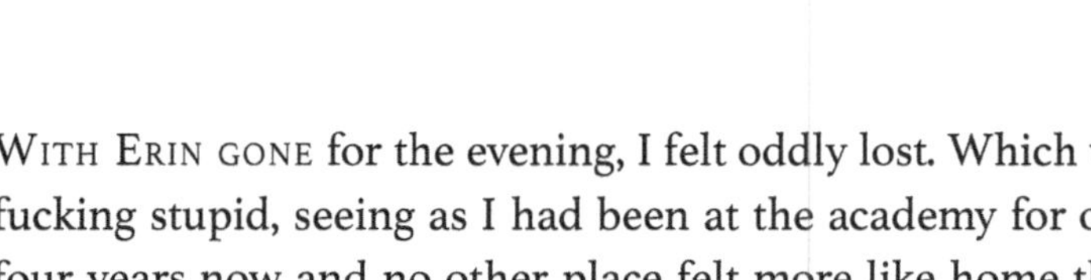

With Erin gone for the evening, I felt oddly lost. Which was fucking stupid, seeing as I had been at the academy for over four years now and no other place felt more like home than here. Well, except for the loft where I had spent the winter break with Erin. That place had been special, but only because she had spent so much time with me there.

One thing kept poking in my mind, bothering me the entire day: how Crimson had let Tom Heyward off with only a warning after attacking Erin with a sword. I believed her when she told me this time she wouldn't let him beat her up like he had done before, but that didn't change the fact that I wanted to teach him a lesson.

Again.

In my raven form, I waited outside the Snapdragon building. As expected, Tom came out later in the evening for a smoke, even though it was freezing cold at this time of night. He walked around the side of the building, where the darkness and shadow of the trees covered it from the paths' views.

I flew down behind the trees, and right before I touched

the ground, I shifted back into my human form. Almost in the same place as the previous time, I rushed into Tom and pressed him against the building's wall, my arm to his throat. The unlit cigarette and lighter fell on the ground.

"What the—?"

I increased the pressure on his neck. "Don't even try. Not this time, you little motherfucker." Two powerful forces warred inside me: one to control my instincts and just scare him again. The other wanted his blood. "You keep on coming for Erin, and I'll skin you alive."

Like a sick vermin, Tom's lips curled up. "I want to see you try." He threw his hand at my chest, and magic hit me hard, sending me skidding back several feet.

"What the fuck?" I stared at him, at his smug expression, at his raised hands, and the knowledge that he had used magic against me. But he wasn't a half-demon, I was sure of that.

"Are you done playing, Reyan?"

What in the ...

Tom's eyes changed and a dark sheen covered even the white space. The eyes of a demon. I sucked in a sharp breath as realization hit me. "You've been possessed."

Tom let out a hollow laugh.

I channeled my magic, ready to hit him with everything I had. Who cared if Tom's body got hurt, as long as I exorcised that damn demon out of him? But before I could use my magic against him, Tom fled, almost as fast as a higher demon.

I stared at the spot where he stood a moment ago, a little taken aback by this new development. One more fucking thing for me to deal with.

I shifted in my raven form and scoured the academy,

looking for Tom, but he was nowhere to be seen. After a couple of hours searching for him, I gave up.

But I didn't forget. I added Tom and his possessed self to my to do list.

I was going to deal with him later.

I HADN'T SLEPT well that night.

After searching for Tom and not finding him, I waited for Erin. She got back to the academy with Claire and Harper late, and I went to her bedroom, where I told her all about Thea and the witches since I hadn't had an opportunity yet, and she told me about her visit to Francine and the new tracking spell.

I also told her about Tom being possessed. She promised to keep an eye on him and avoid being near him for the time being.

After she fell asleep in my arms, I went back to my townhouse. I wished I could spend the night with her, but those twin beds in the dorms didn't really fit the two of us, and I had to stop by my place in the morning anyway, to get ready for class and to be seen there.

But the little I slept was fitful and riddled by nightmares, mostly of Tom being like Tanner, and the demon who had possessed him coming for Erin. Other than that, I even saw my mother and sister in my dreams, both of them dying from the plague and begging me to leave. But in my dreams, they didn't die. They became demons whose purpose was to kill me and my loved ones.

So in the end, I gave up on sleeping and waited for the time to pass.

Despite being exhausted, I was perched atop a tree when Erin left her dorm in the morning and went to the Statice building with Claire and Harper for their first class of the day. And I flew to the Orchid building for my class.

Thankfully, Erin was in my next class and I felt relieved to know she was under the same roof and inside the same walls as me for the next hour, at least. She and Claire took their usual places, the other students arrived and filled the classroom, and I started my lecture.

But five minutes into my class, a bang echoed from the hallway outside. I stilled, wary. Another bang shook the walls and the students gasped.

A shrill scream pierced my ears.

I rushed to the door, the students close behind me, and stepped out in the hallway.

My stomach dropped at the scene.

Tom was on the ground in the middle of the hallway, his stomach open, his insides spread out, and blood splattered everywhere.

On the other side of the scene, Professor Eleanor stared at me with huge eyes. Beside her, Professor Coyne seemed mildly amused with the scene. Behind them, their students were all pale and scared.

The students.

I turned and almost bumped into Erin. "Everyone inside the classroom!" I yelled, ushering them all back into the room. Professor Eleanor did the same with her students.

Professor Coyne, though, didn't seem to care one bit.

As I gently pushed all my students into my classroom, Erin stood close to me. "What the hell?" she whispered.

"I know," I said in a low voice. "Just ... I don't even know."

"Professor Rey!" a new voice resonated through the

hallway. I turned and saw as Crimson walked toward the scene. "If you and Erin Delman will come forward, please."

I stared at Erin for one quick second, before turning to Crimson. As if the news of Tom's death had spread like dust in the wind, the entire faculty showed up at the Orchid building. Professor Ivan walked past us and knelt beside the scene, studying it.

I halted in front of Crimson. "Yes?"

A moment later, Erin showed up at my side.

The headmaster looked at me, then at Erin, as if bored by all of this. "I would assume you two as suspects for this act, but seeing as you were in class at the time with several witness, you two might have either cast a spell to act later, or hired someone."

"What?" Erin squealed.

"You're fucking kidding me," I muttered.

Crimson narrowed his eyes at me. "I expect respect, Professor Rey. That language of yours isn't appropriate."

I clenched my fists, eager to punch him in the fucking nose until it was on the other side of his head.

Professor Ivan stepped back from Tom's body, his nose wrinkled. "This wasn't a simple spell."

Professor Coyne poked at Tom's side with his foot. "This was done by a demon." He lifted his eyes to us, a strange glint in them. "A strong one."

Crimson turned around, addressing everyone, including the students who should have been inside the classrooms, but were spying out. "Everyone go back to your dorms. You are to remain in your buildings for the rest of the day." He clapped his hand hard, making several students jump. "Now, move!"

The students rushed to grab their things and leave the building. In silence, I urged Erin and Claire to do the same.

"I'll catch up with you later," I told her.

Only after the students left the building, Crimson spoke again. "If this was the work of a demon, it means someone let it inside the academy. Because of the increased security, I highly doubt a student did this."

"What are you implying?" Professor Ivan asked, sounding offended.

"That one of you did it and I'll find out who," Crimson said. After a pointed look to each one of us—Coyne snickered at him—Crimson pointed to the nearest door. "Now get out of my sight."

Following his order, the other professors and I walked out of the building. Professor Ivan halted outside and stared back, as if starting a private investigation in his head. Professor Coyne walked away fast, a smug grin on his lips. The other professors huddled together and voiced their concerns for their students.

And I went to the nearest quiet corner, where I shifted into my raven and flew off to check on Erin.

11

BECAUSE OF CRIMSON'S ACCUSATION, I encountered more animosity than normal the next few days. Besides being half-demon, a demonic princess, and user of dark magic, I was now also a murderer. Or so the rumors said.

The day after Tom's death, we still didn't have classes. Instead, a funeral was held, but I wasn't invited. Not that I wanted to go. The guy had brought me nothing but torment. That didn't mean he deserved to die, though.

According to Rey, Crimson was in full investigation mode, doing everything by himself and not letting anyone get involved. Rey also thought Professor Ivan was investigating the murder on his own, while Professor Coyne was acting suspicious by sticking to the corners and laughing when the situation was grim.

Rey wanted to take his turn investigating Tom's murder, mostly to clear our names and have people stop bothering me.

"But I don't want to go down that rabbit hole," he had

said. "It'll only take my focus away from the other problems we have right now."

Which was so damn true, but also unsettling. I might never have liked Tom, but when did we stop caring about others? We hadn't. So I encouraged Rey to investigate if he wanted to.

By the end of the week, he said he hadn't found anything, but probably because Crimson was hiding all the facts. Could the headmaster be involved in this? Was he hiding something?

But as the days went by, we didn't have any answers to our questions.

Worst of all was that, with Tom's murder, the security around the academy tightened even more. Now I couldn't even leave my window open at night. If I did, a guard came by and pounded on my door until I closed the damn window.

My only alternative to see Rey was to teleport to his townhouse, but I only did it twice, because Rey and I were afraid I was still not good at it and I might end up right in front of the guards. And then, in more trouble.

Classes resumed a day after, but the mood was tense as guards stomped through the hallways to make sure no murderer would sneak in and kill another student.

In the meantime, a few parents came to yell at Crimson about the incident and the protection of their kids. Some parents even took their children from school, probably afraid of what this place was turning into.

About ten days after the incident, I was heading to the cafeteria for lunch when I saw Ava alone in the media room. The TV was on, showing a silly show, but Ava's eyes were on the wall beside it, non-seeing.

I sat down beside her, and she almost jumped out of her skin.

"Oh my gosh, are you trying to give me a heart attack?" she complained, straightening up on the couch.

"Sorry," I mumbled. "I just ... wanted to check on you. How are you doing?"

"I'm fine." Eyes on the TV, Ava shrugged. "He was my cousin, but he was a prick and everyone knows it. I'm not saying he deserved what happened to him, but—" She pressed her lips tight for a moment before letting out a long sigh. "I don't know."

Although I was sure she would snap at me, I reached over and placed a hand on her knee. "It's okay to feel conflicted. Like you said, you didn't like him, but he was still your family."

For a moment, I considered telling her he had been possessed and that Rey thought the demon inside of him killed him, but I stopped myself. We weren't sure that was true, and what did it matter to her if he had been possessed? It wouldn't change the fact that her cousin was dead now.

"My father talked to me the other day," she said, her voice low. "He thinks that if things continue as they are, he'll pull me out of the academy." She turned her blue eyes to me. "I don't want to go, but I understand his concern."

I nodded. "I understand it too." My mother had heard about what happened, of course, and she kept texting me every thirty minutes to check on me. It was almost as bad as Rey and his protectiveness. With Rey, I found it sexy most of the time. With my mother, it was annoying. "He's saying that because he loves you."

She snorted. "His ways of showing that are a little unorthodox."

"Hey, hm, I'm going to the cafeteria for dinner," I said, trying to drag her out of her own mind. "Want to come with me?"

Ava wrinkled her nose. "No, I'm not hungry."

I waited a minute more, thinking what I could say to her, but nothing seemed appropriate, so I got up and left. With a heavy feeling weighing on me, I went to the cafeteria where I met Claire and Harper for dinner.

"THIS SHOULD WORK," Harper said, lighting the candles on my desk. "Just stay there, breathe deeply, and relax."

Seated with my legs crossed in the middle of my room, I stared at her. "Do you know me?"

Harper chuckled. "I do, but I also know you're determined and stubborn. If you force yourself to relax, you will."

Well, when she put it that way ...

I glanced around my bedroom. During dinner earlier, Claire and Harper had convinced me that if I waited for the perfect time to use the scrying spell Francine had taught me, I would never do it. Quiet place and being relaxed? That didn't exist, not for me, at least. So we had to create the mood. Harper got some scented candles, and Claire closed the curtains to create a dim atmosphere.

Then, they pushed me down on the floor and spread the map in front of me.

Next, they handed me the crystal and a needle.

"What else do you need?" Claire asked.

"How about some soft ballads to help with the mood?" Harper asked.

"No, no songs," I said. This was ridiculous. With their

eagerness rubbing on me, it would be much too difficult for me to focus and relax.

Though, I had to admit, the soft cinnamon scent from the candles was a nice touch.

I shifted my weight, straightened my back, and closed my eyes.

I thought of cinnamon, starry night skies, sea waves, romantic candlelight dinners ... I tried clearing my mind, and not thinking of anything else other than those things. In no time, my mind was blank and my breathing even.

Who knew this relaxing technique worked?

Trying to keep myself calm, I opened my eyes. Slowly, I pricked the tip of my index finger with the needle and let a fat drop fall on the center of the map. It disappeared instantly, just like Francine said it would.

I handed the needle to the girls and focused on the crystal in my hand, and on my magic. I tried to play with it, to dance with it, to follow its waves and power, as if it were colorful, swirly lines around me. I focused on my blood, on the part of it that also belonged to my siblings.

I stared at the map.

Nothing happened.

I frowned. "Maybe I'm not as relaxed as I tho—" The rest of my sentence died on my lips as small red dots appeared on the map. A dozen, two dozen, a hundred, several hundred red dots all over the globe. "Holy shit."

"I guess Brikan has been busy," Claire muttered, her tone tight, as if she was mad at my father for getting around.

I confess that bothered me a little too. But more than that ... "For now, I only need to find the two who have the same mark as me. How will I ever narrow this down?"

"Try your magic," Harper suggested.

"Yes," Claire agreed. "Just, I don't know, think about what you want. Since the crystal answered your first question, it might do it again."

I nodded and focused on the crystal again. First, I eliminated all the people who were too young or too old to participate in a war. Hopefully, the ones with the mark weren't in those groups. Second, I eliminated all the males, since the prophecy was about queens, not kings. Next, I requested to see only the ones in the immediate area, where we could drive or teleport.

Magically, the map zoomed in on the region, and only three dots remained on the map. All of them were about an hour from here.

"What now?" I muttered, my mind reeling. Holy shit, I had done it! I had found my half-siblings.

"What do you mean, what now?" Claire grabbed my arm and hoisted me up. "You go find them!"

I glanced at my phone. It was past nine at night. There was only one way I could go after them right now.

One corner of my lips curled up. "I guess I'll have to teleport to Rey's townhouse."

Harper shot me a knowing glance. "What a torture."

I winked at her, then teleported away.

I appeared in Rey's living room. I turned around, expecting to see him raiding the fridge for more ice cream, but he wasn't here. Only the cabinet lights were on, giving the place an eerie glow.

"Rey?" I called, walking to the stairs.

Then, I heard it. The faint sound of water running. He was in the shower. Biting my lower lip, I tiptoed up the stairs and into his bedroom. I spied in the bathroom, and sure enough, he was in the shower.

Feeling a little bold, I took off my clothes. I spied again. When he raised his head to the shower, with his eyes closed, I rushed into the shower with him.

"Whoa," he said, taking a step back. He opened his eyes and saw it was me. "Despite the scare you just gave me, this is a nice surprise." He wrapped his arms around me, gluing his rock hard body against mine, and brought me under the warm water. "To what do I owe this visit?"

Bringing my arms around his shoulders, I shrugged. "Is it that uncommon for me to show up here?"

"In my shower, yes." A small smile curved his lips. "I was going to your room later."

"I know. I just had to tell you something I found out."

"Is it important?"

"It is, yes. Why?"

"Because if it can wait—" He spun us around and pushed me against the cold, tiled wall. "—there's a more pressing issue I would like to discuss first."

Rey pressed his body against mine, and his head dipped into my throat. I gasped as heat coursed through me. Butterflies danced in my stomach, and my legs gave out. "I ... I think it can wait," I breathed out, barely remembering what I had to tell him.

He pulled back slightly and looked into my eyes. "Good."

Then, he claimed my mouth and my body.

***

AFTER A FUN TIME in the shower, somehow, Rey and I made it to his bed, and miraculously, we didn't get everything in our path wet. He held on to me as we both relaxed and let sleep come to us. But how could I sleep when I was wrapped around his naked body?

Rey ran his hand up and down my back. "What was it that you wanted to tell me?"

"What?" I raised my head to look at him. Oh, shit, I had almost forgotten why I had come here. "Oh, I did the spell. With the map and the crystal."

His body tensed under me, and suddenly, Rey was all business again. "And?"

"I found three of my siblings within an hour from here."

"Really?"

I nodded. "I'm surprised too. You should have seen it. Before I started narrowing it down, there were hundreds of dots."

"Wow." Rey's brows pinched. "I guess we should go check on these people."

"I think so too." I reached for my phone and glanced at the time. It was almost midnight. "I guess it's pretty late now, though."

"I don't have any classes tomorrow morning, and I know you're not against skipping, so ..."

"We should go see them tomorrow morning," I said, a little anxious about this new mission.

"That's what I thought."

"I'm in," I said, snuggling into him again and burying my head on his shoulder. "Now, let me sleep."

I felt his chuckle rumbling on his chest. I loved being here with him, feeling him with me like this, pretending we were happy and carefree all the time. I just wished that after all we were gearing up to face, we could actually live like this.

This was my biggest wish.

12

———

As a professor, some rules were more lenient for me, like leaving the academy grounds. After breakfast, I drove past the gates, and about a mile down the main road, I pulled over and waited.

Not ten minutes later, Erin showed up from behind the trees. Per our plan, she teleported from her dorm room. Boots sinking in the snow, she trudged to my car and slipped inside with a shiver.

"Damn, it's cold." She rubbed her hands together.

"Everything okay?"

She nodded. "Claire said she would tell the professors I wasn't feeling great."

"Let's hope no one checks on you."

Erin stretched her hands in front of the hot air coming out of the vents. "Let's hope Claire will intervene and say she'll check on me for them."

I turned the wheel and started driving again, taking us away from the academy. Erin synced her phone with my car's system and put on a rock station. She nodded her head along with the song, and I suddenly never felt more human.

Just her and me, driving down an empty road, under the rising sun, like a normal road trip. I glanced at her and inhaled deeply. Her beauty always took my breath away. I loved everything about her. Her long, luscious black hair, her smooth skin, the freckles on her delicate nose, her red lips, her shiny golden eyes, her hot, hot body, and everything else in between. She touched my soul like nothing else in the world, and I couldn't imagine living another thousand years without her.

Though, I wasn't sure I would live that long anymore. Asmodeus had gifted me immortality when we made our deal. It wasn't as if I couldn't die, I just hadn't aged.

Until now. It had been over a year since Randall had killed Asmodeus, and I was pretty sure the clock had restarted for me once our deal was broken. I would only be able to confirm it in a couple of years, when I saw and felt the difference, but I was pretty sure.

Which meant I could grow old with Erin.

I reached across the seats and took her hand in mine, entwining our fingers together. I brought her hand to my mouth and kissed the top gently, then settled our joined hands on my lap.

Erin brought one leg over the seat and folded it under herself, turning slightly toward me. "What is it?"

"Just thinking," I muttered.

"About?"

"Us."

"Hmm, I like that. What about us?"

I stole another glance at her. "Our future. Once this is all said and done. What will we do, where will we be … that kind of stuff."

"I don't know what we'll be doing and where we'll be, but if I survive what's coming for me, I know one thing for sure: I'll be with you."

I wanted to argue with her about the "if" in her sentence, but I was just buying an argument I wouldn't win. Instead, I brought her hand to my lips and kissed her knuckles again.

"I wish we didn't have to hide," I whispered.

"Me too, but I keep in mind that it's only until I graduate. That's a little over a year."

Or, if it happened before her graduation, until we defeated Brikan and Erin was safe. Once I knew she was safe, I could quit being a professor and become a full-fledged demon hunter. Though, thinking about it now, I realized I would probably stay at the academy with her, even after that, because I wanted to be close to her. Once she graduated, then I would follow her wherever she wanted to go.

We continued with small talk for the rest of the ride, but too fucking soon, we arrived at our destination. The first spot on the map took us to a small town on the other side of the mountain. As we got closer, the map in Erin's lap zoomed in, showing us the streets in town. It was almost like our own witchy GPS.

Finally, we parked the car on the red dot: a small house with a huge lot on a not-so friendly side of town. With peeling paint, broken siding and broken roof, dust and cobwebs around the porch, the house looked abandoned.

Erin eyed the map. "This can't be right."

"We're already here," I said, unbuckling my seat belt. "I say let's check it out."

We exited my car and stepped into the snow-covered

driveaway. If someone lived here, then they hadn't left the house in at least three days—that was when we had the last snowfall in this area.

We were halfway through the driveway when a darkfire bolt zipped from the house and grazed Erin's shoulder, burning off a piece of her jacket.

"What the fuck?" I raised my hands, bringing a wall of darkfire in front of us, just as another bolt came for me.

It bounced off the shield and died on the snow.

"Who's there?" I asked, holding the shield up, but not advancing.

"We're not going to hurt you," Erin shouted. "We just want to talk."

A young girl, not older than seventeen, sneaked half of her body outside the house, her dark curls falling to the side. "Go away!"

"No, no." Erin tucked the folded map on her packet and quickly raised her hands as a sign of peace. She shot me a glare. "Lower the damn shield." I groaned, not liking this idea, but let my magic go. The shield disappeared.

"Just go away," the girl said. "Whatever you got to say, we don't want to hear."

"We?" I said in a low voice.

Erin looked at me. She picked up the map from her pocket and unfolded it. The map zoomed in over the house and showed three red spots. "Holy shit," she said. Holding on to the map, Erin took two steps forward. "You might not believe me, but ... I'm your sister, and I really would like an opportunity to talk to you."

The girl frowned. Slowly, she stepped out onto the porch, wearing a thin shirt and ripped jeans. She crossed her arms. "Then talk."

Erin let out a long sigh. This wasn't going too well.

"Where's your mother?" I asked. Perhaps talking with the one in charge would make things easier. Maybe she and her siblings didn't know who their father was.

Another girl stepped out of the house, her dark curls bouncing as she dragged her bare feet to the edge of the porch. She was as badly dressed as her older sister. "She died a couple of months ago," the girl said. "A demon killed her."

I frowned. "You killed the demon?"

The girl nodded. "The three of us together, but we couldn't save our mother."

"I'm sorry," Erin whispered. I was sure she was remembering her aunt, Paula, who had died trying to save her from demons.

"I'm Kristin," the girl said. "What's your name?"

"I'm Erin." Erin gestured to me. "And this is Rey."

"The grumpy one is Karen, and the one spying through the window," Kristin pointed to the window a couple of feet to the side, "is Katrina."

"How old are you?" I asked, worried.

"I'm twelve, Karen is seventeen, and Katrina is fifteen," Kristin said.

This wasn't right. Three girls underaged left alone in a rotting house. "Why are you here alone? Don't you have any relatives to take care of you?"

"We do—"

"Enough with the questions," Karen snapped, interrupting Kristin. "You said you're our sister. How do you know that?"

"I used a magical spell to find you," Erin said, being honest.

"Why were you looking for us?" Karen asked.

She really wasn't going easy on us. Which was good. If she was the oldest, I hoped she was tough enough to protect the others. Still, the three of them alone wasn't right.

"I wanted to talk to you about our father," Erin answered. "Do you know anything about him?"

"Yes!" Kristin answered. For a twelve-year-old who had just lost her mother and lived in terrible conditions, she was pretty friendly and happy. "Our mother told us about him. His name is Brikan and he's the king of the under realm."

"Underworld," Karen corrected her.

"Right." Kristin nodded. "The underworld. Our mother told us he's a bad man, and if he ever came for us, we should run."

Karen slapped her hand on Kristin's shoulder. "Shut up. You're saying too much."

"She's our sister," Kristin protested.

A chilly breeze blew around us. Soon, Erin and I would be icicles in the snow, but I knew Erin preferred being cold to forcing herself upon them. Kristin's hair whipped across her face and she raised her hand to brush the strands back. The long sleeve of her thin shirt fell to her elbows, revealing her wrist.

My breath caught and Erin gasped.

We shared a glance.

"Kristin, I have this tattoo too." Erin folded the sleeve of her jacket and showed the mark to them. "Do you know what that means?" Kristin shook her head. Erin took another step toward them. "It means we have a special mission. We have to unite and fight Brikan. Only the ones with the mark will be able to defeat him."

Kristin's hazel eyes bugged.

"No, that's bullshit," Karen said. "And even if it was true, forget it. Kristin will never join you and fight the king of the underworld. That's just nuts."

"I understand your reservations. I mean, she's only twelve. In your place, I wouldn't have allowed it either, but ... you have to consider that Brikan knows who has this mark—" Erin lifted her wrist. "—and sooner or later, he'll come for us. He'll kill us if we don't kill him first."

"Stop it!" Karen grabbed Kristin's shoulders and steered her into the house. "Everything you're saying, it's absurd. And even if it's true and he comes for Kristin, I won't let him hurt her."

"Just ..." Erin reached for them, but stopped herself. "I know it's a long shot, but in case you change your mind, here's my number." She offered Karen a card. The oldest sister didn't take it, so Erin left it on the porch floor. Hopefully, the wind wouldn't blow it away. "His number is there too," she said, gesturing to me. "You can call us any time."

"It won't happen." Karen disappeared into the house and slammed the door.

I wound an arm around Erin's shoulder and pulled her to me. "It's okay. We did what we could. For now." I turned her around and steered her toward my car. "We'll think of something, but first let's get out of this cold."

Once inside my car, Erin stared at me, her eyes round. "I just asked a twelve-year-old to join me in a war against the most powerful being that ever existed. Can I blame her sister for shutting me down? Of course not. I'm insane. Completely insane."

I cupped her face. "You might be insane, but you're insane for the right reasons." I pressed my lips to hers in a quick kiss. "Just ... forget about this for now. We'll worry about it tomorrow."

I drove away, and Erin lay back on the passenger seat. She stared out the window, and remained quiet the rest of the ride back to the academy. As much as I wanted to drive to the next red dot on the map, I thought Erin could handle only so much heartbreak for one day. Besides, I had a class to teach this afternoon, and I couldn't have Crimson more suspicious of me than he already was. If I disappeared without explanation, he would use that against me.

But I couldn't lie to myself. I was feeling pretty fucking defeated myself.

What would we do if one of the Demon Kissed Queens couldn't join us?

13

ERIN

I HAD THOUGHT that after finding my siblings, all the pieces would start falling into place, and things would work out. I had never expected for one of the Demon Kissed Queens to be a twelve-year-old girl. How could I expect her to join me in battle? And I had even told her to call us if she changed her mind. I was freaking insane.

Rey and I had plans to find the next red dot on the map the next day, but Crimson realized I was missing classes. He sent me an official school letter saying that if I missed more classes, be it for being sick or whatever, I would face disciplinary action.

All I needed was more attention and trouble, so I stayed put and attended all my classes, despite barely paying attention to them.

A few days later, during Defense Against Demons, Professor Ivan noticed I kept messing up my assignment, and he stopped me again as I was leaving the classroom.

Claire signaled me that she would be going to our next class, then I approached Professor Ivan's desk. "Did I do something wrong?" I asked, afraid he too would bother me about missing classes and being easily distracted.

Seated behind his desk, the professor glanced at me, his brows curled down. "Is everything okay? You seem troubled."

I stared at the professor. He was a famous demon hunter and he had been nothing but kind to me. He was probably wise and knew a lot of things about the supernatural world I couldn't even imagine. For a moment, I considered telling him. The prophecy, Fiona, my siblings, Tanner ... everything.

But I didn't. I didn't because I already had a large and trusted support group. Rey, Claire, and Harper had my back, no matter what. If I called, I knew Ava and Harvey would help me too. And there was also my mother. She might be a tough cookie, but I knew she cared about me and would do anything to protect me.

And I didn't trust him, not completely. How could I if I barely knew him?

"I've been worried about the Shadow Trials," I told him, which wasn't a lie. "I have no idea what to expect, how to prepare for it, and that has been keeping me up at night."

"I understand." He entwined his fingers over his desk. "To be honest, I don't know much about the Shadow Trials either. The headmaster hasn't told us a lot, other than it'll be a deadly contest with many phases." He tsked. "Sorry, I can't help you with that."

"It's fine." I offered him a small, friendly smile. "When the time comes, I'll just improvise."

"I'm sure you'll be fine," he said, sounding confident.

"Thanks." I raised my hand in a wave. "I'll see you later."

"Bye, Erin," he muttered as I walked out of the classroom.

In the hallway, I turned to the right, to go to my next class, and came to a halt when I almost bumped into Professor

Coyne, who was leaning against the wall, his arms crossed and a sneer on his lips.

"Oh, I'm sorry." I stepped back.

He didn't say anything. He just watched me with his dark eyes, as if he knew a secret I didn't, as I hurried down the hallway and away from him. What a creep!

Entering my next class, I saw Claire in our usual spot in the center, and Harvey to the right. I remembered about wanting to talk to him. I glanced at my wristwatch. We still had five minutes before the next class started, so I lifted my index finger to Claire, silently telling her to wait, and sat down next to Harvey.

"Erin, hey," he said, surprised to see me. "Everything okay?"

"Sort of." I shrugged. "Always the same problems. How about you?"

He narrowed his eyes at me. "What's going on?"

"You tell me," I said. "Ava has been really cranky lately, and I think it's because of you."

"I didn't do anything!"

"And that's the problem." I leaned in closer, so no one could hear us. "Don't you like her? I thought you did, in your own way."

"I used to," he confessed in a low voice. "For the longest time, I thought our parents were right and we would end up together. But as we grew up, she became clingy and jealous, and we weren't even dating."

"You know she feels like you're keeping a leash on her," I told him. "Like you want her, but you don't reel her in, so she's there, just waiting for you."

He let out a long sigh. "I never meant to do that to her."

"Then you need to let her know," I told him. "If you're

really not into her, you need to tell her. That's the only way she'll let go of you and move on."

Harvey furrowed his brow, but didn't say anything.

I was going to nag him some more, but the professor walked into the classroom, and I went to my place beside Claire.

"What was that about?" she asked in a whisper.

I frowned, thinking about Rey and me. Rey had been somewhat like Harvey last semester. He said he didn't want to be with me, but he ended up kissing me several times, reeling me in. Just to push me away again.

I sighed. "I told him that if he doesn't want to date Ava, he has to let Ava go."

"Oh, that's not gonna be pretty," she said.

I nodded. "I know."

Then, the professor greeted us and started the class, and I tried paying attention for once.

14

REY

ERIN and I had planned to go after her other siblings on the weekend, but when the time came, the red dots disappeared from the map. It was like the tracking spell's validity had expired.

Saturday afternoon, she spread candles around the empty living room of my townhouse, sat down on the cold floor right in the center of the room, and tried performing the spell again.

A minute later, she groaned. "I can't do it. Harper's grandmother said I should be in a quiet place and totally relaxed to do this. I certainly don't feel relaxed now."

"Want me to leave?" I asked from the kitchen island. I kept my distance, so I wouldn't bother her, or taint the spell.

"No, it's not you." She pushed to her feet again. "It's everything else. Kristin, Tom's death, the accusations, the Shadow Trials." She ticked her fingers, counting the many things. "There's a lot more. Shall I go on?"

I walked to her. "No, I get it. Your mind isn't into it."

She let out a long breath. "But I have to find a way to relax. I need to find them again."

I wound my arms around her and pulled her to me. "Perhaps it isn't you. Perhaps it's just the spell that is gone for real."

She looked up at me. "But if it's gone for real, how am I going to find the other Demon Kissed Queen?"

I smoothed my hands down her long hair. "I don't know. But don't give up hope just yet. We found one. We'll find the other one." But I knew Erin was also disappointed about Kristin. Not the that girl was to blame, but she was too young. Erin didn't want to drag her down a doomed path. I kissed her forehead. "What shall I do to help you relax?"

Erin turned her head and rested her cheek on my chest. "Hm, how about taking me to the bedroom and making love to me?"

Holy fuck. Didn't she know by now how weak I was when it came to her? With a growl, I scooped her in my arms. "As you wish."

I took two steps toward the stairs when Erin's phone beeped. She waved her hand at it, silently telling me to ignore it. After two more steps, her phone beeped again. A second later, mine beeped too.

We stared at each other. What the fuck could this be? I gently dropped Erin on her feet and we both got our phones from the kitchen island.

"It's Ava," she said.

"It's Harvey," I told her, reading his text.

Harvey: *What are you up to?*

My phone beeped again.

Harvey: *Don't tell me you're with Erin. Ditch her and let's do something with the guys.*

I frowned. What guys? Besides Harvey, I didn't have any male friends, and I knew Peter had been Harvey's best friend, but he was gone now.

Me: *You mean just you and me.*

Harvey: *And a bottle of whiskey. I snatched several from my house before coming back to the academy.*

I glanced at Erin as she texted Ava on her phone. I didn't want to leave her, but I felt bad about Harvey.

"Harvey wants to do something," I told her.

"Ava wants that too." She looked up from her phone, meeting my eyes. "She said she got Claire and Harper in the media room, and they want to crack open a wine bottle."

Harvey with whiskey, Ava with wine. Soon, we would have a party going on.

Erin's phone beeped. She sighed as she read the message. "Ava is saying she'll find where the theater room is this semester and instead of watching a movie, she'll start a party."

My phone rang.

Harvey: *Ava is starting a party in the theater room. You're going with me.*

I gaped at my phone.

Me: *How do you already know that?*

Harvey: *How do YOU know about that?*

I looked up at Erin. "All right, this is fucking messed up. Harvey already knows about this theater room party."

Erin rolled her eyes. "Ava must be texting several people and setting up the party." Her phone rang again. "And now it's Claire, saying Ava is depressed. We need to have a party for her. Need is in capital letters."

Harvey and Ava ... these two were dramatic.

Ava needed Erin, and Harvey needed me, but now I was a

fucking professor. I couldn't end up at this party and mixed up with the other students. Even if I went against rules and showed up there to support Harvey, it would be hell, because I wouldn't be able to be near Erin.

But there was a place we could be just us.

"Tell Ava, Claire, and Harper to be ready," I said to Erin. "We're leaving in ten minutes."

SINCE ERIN WANTED to change clothes and apply some makeup, it took us thirty minutes to leave the academy instead of ten. But when I told them I would take them to an underground club, they stopped complaining and waited patiently.

First, Erin teleported to Harvey's room, where she got him, then she teleported to Claire's room, where the rest of our group waited for us.

"Everyone hold hands," Erin said. Claire put herself between Harvey and Ava before they started bickering and held their hands. When the circle was closed, Erin teleported us to the edge of the forest.

Unfortunately, because she didn't have much practice, her jumps weren't the longest, but with my borrowed magic, she didn't get too tired as she took us jump by jump to Denver.

I guided her until we were in a not-so-good neighborhood. Once we were close enough, I told everyone to follow me.

Harvey fell into step with me. "I thought this shit would be just you and me."

"Just ignore the others," I told him. "The place is big enough. You can pretend they aren't there."

Harvey groaned, muttering curses, but I let it slide. To me, it seemed he was down not only because of his friends' loss, but something else too. I glanced at Ava. She was beside Erin, chattering away. Like Harvey, she was probably complaining about this outing.

"Where is this place?" Claire asked, following us. She glanced around, clearly wary of where we were.

"We're close," I told her. A minute later, I gestured to an open parking lot in front of an abandoned store. I opened the broken door. "Through here."

Erin narrowed her eyes at me. "What is this place?"

"You'll see." I slipped my hand in hers and squeezed it tight.

Once everyone was inside the abandoned building, I took them to the hallway and down a staircase. A door met us at the end of the staircase. I knocked on it.

The door opened, revealing a big man with a mohawk and dozens of piercings around his ears. He stared at us, as if waiting for something.

I lifted my hand, turned my open palm up, and conjured darkfire.

The man grunted and stepped aside.

We filed inside a small rectangle room and waited by the only other door. The man then unlocked the door. I twisted the knob and pushed it open.

The electronic music echoed in my ears and lights blinked.

"Welcome to the demon underground," I told Erin and the others as we stepped into the hidden club.

Holding on to Erin's hand, I guided our group down the wide stairs to the main area of the club: a big, open area, now filled with demons as they danced to the pounding music.

The DJ was on a small stage to the right, there were tall tables and chairs in the back, and a large bar was on the left. A second floor balcony wrapped around the entire place with private VIP sections.

Erin leaned into me and said close to my ear, "These are all demons?"

I nodded. "Most of them, at least. I bet there are other supernaturals who come here for fun." Like we were doing right now.

"What if we're caught?" she asked, sounding worried.

"The club rules state that no one should be harmed while in the facilities, no matter what they are," I told her. Of course, the rules had been broken before, and I had actually witnessed a witch kill a vampire once. Since then, the security had increased tenfold. Besides demons monitoring everything up close, there were dozens of cameras and spells in place to prevent anything like that from happening again.

Harvey approached me. "I'm going to get a drink."

I nodded, but he didn't even see me as he dragged his feet to the bar. Maybe coming here hadn't been a good idea.

Ava was the second one at the bar, ordering tequila.

"If we don't do something, this idea will turn south," Erin said, her eyes on both Ava and Harvey.

I decided to do more. Leaving Erin with Claire and Harper, I went up to the VIP balconies. There were a few sections unoccupied. After talking to one of the security guards and paying a nice sum, I secured a balcony space for us. I ordered several drinks and appetizers and had it delivered to our section while I went to retrieve Erin and the others.

"Come with me," I told them. Erin, Claire, Harper, and

Ava followed me right away. I had to glare at Harvey and grab his arm to make him come with us.

When we entered the balcony—a square area with low velvet couches and tables and a railing overlooking the dance floor—the girls went crazy. They attacked the food and drinks and began dancing.

Harvey picked up a whiskey glass, flopped down on a corner of the couch, and glared at me. What? Was he mad at me? He had been the one to invite me to a party. This one was better, at least.

Ignoring him, I grabbed a beer from the table, popped the cap open, took a long, chilling swallow, and watched my girl. Erin had mixed a little Coke in her whiskey, and now she danced with Claire, Harper, and Ava, her body undulating and moving to the beat of the music.

Heat spread low in my body and I licked my lips. Fuck, this was hot. She was fucking hot.

In the VIP area to our left, some guys noticed the girls and started watching them. All right, that was it. They could watch Claire, Harper, and Ava, but they could not watch Erin.

After another long sip of my beer, I went to her.

She spun in place, turning her back to me.

I stepped into her, gluing my body to hers, and wound my arm around her tiny waist. I lowered my head to her shoulder. "Hi, gorgeous."

She glanced at me, a naughty smile in her lips.

Fuck.

We should have stayed in my townhouse. More specifically, in my bed.

In no time, Ava was flirting with the guys, Claire and Harper danced, though Claire kept on checking out the guys talking to Ava, and Harper scowled at them, clearly upset about the attention Claire was getting from those guys. Claire was really clueless to Harper's feelings.

Harvey sulked, drinking a lot and watching Ava. But when I told him to man up and go talk to her, he dismissed me.

And Erin and I drank and danced and kissed, not necessarily in that order. Though I had been the one to suggest coming here, I hadn't really felt like it. I just wanted to offer an alternative to what was offered to me. But now that we were here, I liked it. It was nice to hold Erin in the middle of a crowd of people—or demons—and not care who saw us and what they thought about it.

Drunk from the beer and from her, I cupped her face and kissed her deep and long. Erin molded her body to mine, but continued moving her hips, rubbing against me. Heat spread through my body, and I swallowed a growl. It was all I could do not to throw her on the couch and ravage her right here.

Breathing hard, Erin broke the kiss. "We should stop before we're escorted out of here."

I locked my arms around her, not letting her go anywhere. "I bet they would like a show."

Erin punched my shoulder. "That's so not my thing."

I knew that, but it was fun to tease her. I also knew she was right. If we didn't stop now, we weren't stopping at all, so I reined in my desire and took a large step back from her.

She pouted at me.

"What? If you want me to stop, you need to be away from me," I said, grabbing my almost empty beer bottle. I finished it in one swallow and inhaled deeply, trying to clear my mind from Erin and everything else about her.

I took another step back and glanced around.

A beautiful woman with long red hair strolled past the

VIP sections. I narrowed my eyes and watched as she smiled at a man in another VIP couch and he practically became goo at her feet.

The woman was already several steps away when she raised her hand and flipped her hair back.

I stilled, staring at her wrist.

The demon kissed mark.

She had the demon kissed mark.

"Erin." I reached for her and pointed to the woman. "She has the mark on her wrist." Erin blinked as if not hearing me. I turned her arm around and pointed to her wrist. "This mark. She has this mark."

Erin's eyes widened.

Half a second later, she ran out of our VIP section and went after the woman. I followed her, but as soon as we arrived at the edge of the stairs, a large group of people came up, stepping in our way and delaying our progress.

By the time Erin and I made it downstairs, we had lost the woman.

"Where did she go?" Erin asked, looking around.

Being taller than Erin, I tried spotting the red hair in the crowd, but besides it being dark in here, the woman wasn't that tall. She could easily be lost in the throng.

A waiter holding a round tray stopped in front of us. "Are you looking for something?"

"For someone," Erin said. "A redheaded woman and—"

The waiter nodded. "No need to say more. I know who she is. Her name is Jasmin."

"You know her?" I asked. "Where can we find her?"

"I know *of* her," the waiter said. "Everyone who works in the club knows of her. She comes here often, but disappears as fast as she comes. To be honest, several of my colleagues are obsessed with her. I mean, can you blame them? She's gorgeous, but she never lets anyone get too close."

I frowned. "And no one knows her phone number?"

The waiter shook his head. "Nope."

Someone flagged the waiter. He excused himself and went to see what the customer wanted.

Erin turned to me. "What do we do now?"

"We can continue looking for her around the club," I suggested. "But if we don't find her, the only thing I can think of is to try and use the map again, see if we can spot her around here."

"We better get going, then." Erin slipped her hand in mine and we both went back to the VIP area. We leaned over the railing and looked over the dance floor and surrounding areas, but we only spotted two other red-haired people, and they were different from the woman we had seen earlier.

We spent hours waiting to see her around the club, to no avail.

Our only hope now was to try the map scrying again.

15

ERIN

I SPENT most of Sunday trying to find my red-haired sister with the map, but again, it didn't work. I made a mental note to ask Harper when I saw her later for her grandmother's number, so I could ask the old woman what was happening. Was the map out of juice, or did it have a limited time of use?

But Rey had a better idea: just before nighttime, I teleported us both to the club. We arrived as the staff was finishing cleaning the place up to open it for the night.

At first, the bouncer didn't want us to come inside, but Rey smooth-talked him, and we were allowed in. I gawked around as we went down the steps, amazed at how this place looked totally different with the lights on, without music, and without the crowd. It was large, clean, and almost boring.

"You two," a voice said.

We turned to the bar and found the waiter from last night putting some glasses away.

"Hi," I said, approaching him. "We were wondering if you or someone else could answer a few questions about Jasmin."

The waiter frowned. "I'll call my boss. Wait here." He left through an opening behind the bar.

Rey and I took two high stools in front of the bar and waited.

Not a minute later, the waiter was back, and a tall man in a dark blue suit appeared with him.

"I'm Matt, the owner of this place," he said, offering his hand to us. "What can I do for you?"

Rey and I quickly shook his hand.

"We are looking for Jasmin," Rey said, directly to the point.

"Everyone is looking for Jasmin," Matt said with a scoff.

I frowned. "What do you mean?"

"I mean, she's a mystery." He reached for a whiskey glass and put some ice in it. "She frequents the club all the time and goes home with a different man each night. Which I'm not complaining. Honestly, I like it. A lot of men who have heard about her come here trying to find her. I tried talking to her about working for me, but like everyone else, she didn't spare me two seconds."

Was she some kind of prostitute? "Do you know where she lives? Or where she works?"

Matt shook his head as he poured some whiskey on his glass. "That's part of the mystery. I know Denver is a big city, but I know *a lot* of people, and I have never seen Jasmin other than inside this club." He leaned in closer and said, "Some people say she's a ghost." He chuckled at his joke.

"Someone must know more about her," Rey mused.

"All I know is that a lot of people tried getting closer to her, to find out more about her, and failed. She remains a mystery."

We tried asking more questions, but they all lead to the

same answer: Matt and the club staff didn't know shit about Jasmin besides her name and the fact that she always left with a different man.

Discouraged, Rey and I went back to the academy, where I tried using the map one more time.

Nothing.

This was going from bad to worse.

***

On Monday, I overslept and rushed to class. On my way to the Orchid building on the other side of the campus, I bumped into Ava.

"Are you late too?" I asked, falling into step with her.

"Yup," she said, her long legs working in her favor. I wasn't short by any means, but I wasn't as tall as Ava either.

I hadn't seen her all day yesterday and was dying to ask her something. "So, I saw you flirting with those guys from the VIP seats beside ours," I started, my voice careful. Sometimes she shut me out when I least expected her to. "Was all that a show to make Harvey jealous?"

"Yes, and no," she said, looking straight ahead. "I think it started that way, but then I realized there are plenty of fish in the tank. I don't need to just stand here and wait for him to change his mind. I can go out and try to find someone for me, someone who likes me and my craziness. Hopefully, I'll find a nice guy and I'll fall in love and forget all about Harvey."

"Well, I'm a little sad because I already had you two as an item in my head, but at the same time, I'm happy that you're taking charge of things and moving on." I leaned into her and bumped my shoulder on hers. "You go, girl."

She snickered. "What about you and Rey? I always knew

you two liked each other, but I think that was the first time I actually saw you two together, and well, you are together together. There were moments there I feared we would see more than needed."

I chuckled as we went up the front stairs of the Orchid building. "Yeah, we are together together, finally. And we'll stay like that forever."

She raised an eyebrow at me. "What? Are you two soulmates?" She asked in a teasing tone, but only because she didn't know about the soul bond. It occurred to me that it was odd that Ava didn't know about it. She and I had an odd relationship, but for some reason, I thought that, by now, she knew everything about me.

I opened my mouth to tell her about it—no reason why not—when someone appeared right in front of us.

I skidded to a stop, almost slipping on a small patch of ice left in the ground. "Yes?" I asked the woman in our path. She was one of Crimson's secretaries.

"The headmaster would like to see you, Ms. Erin," she said, sounding like a robot.

"Right now?" I pointed to the building behind her. "I have class in two minutes."

"Right now, Ms. Erin," she said.

"What about me?" Ava asked.

The secretary didn't look her way as she said, "You can go to class, Ms. Ava." She stepped back and gestured to the path that led to the Aster building. "This way, Ms. Erin."

I shrugged at Ava, then turned and followed the secretary-robot to the Aster building. On the way, I asked her what was this about, but of course, she didn't say a word. Probably because she didn't know, but even if she did, she didn't look like the kind to spill the beans so easily.

My stomach knotted. What could Crimson want with me now? For him to call me right when I had class, it was probably a big thing.

The secretary knocked on the door of Crimson's new office.

"Come in," his voice boomed from the inside.

The secretary opened the door and gestured for me to walk in. Once I stepped inside, she closed the door behind me.

And I faced Crimson in Randall's office. Once more, he surprised me by not changing everything. As far as I knew, he had hated Randall. Why leave everything intact, then? If I ever occupied the office of someone I hated, I would change every single inch of it.

Seated on the big armchair behind the desk, Crimson offered me a tight smile. "Ms. Erin, sorry for disrupting your class. Don't worry, I warned the professor you'll be late."

"What's the matter?" I asked, willing my voice to sound polite.

Crimson extended his hand over his desk. "I need you to hand over your Dawnblade."

I gaped at him. "W-what?"

"I know you have a special Dawnblade, like the one Randall had," he said, the creepy smile still on his lips, though his eyes shone with disgust. I knew he didn't like half-demons, but he was the damn headmaster of this academy. He too had to respect the students, no matter what they were. "A lot of people saw you sporting the sword last semester. Such a sword is dangerous and powerful."

I gulped. So what? He wanted it for himself? "If you saw it then, why are you asking for it only now?"

"The school board wanted to confiscate the Dawnblade

from you right away," he said. "But I told them I didn't see why. But now I remembered about the Shadow Trials. Soon, it'll be time for the contest, and I can't let you have a powerful weapon. It'll be unfair to the other students. As half-demons, they don't even have a Dawnblade to begin with."

I frowned, thinking of Rey. He had a Dawnblade and he was a half-demon too. But I wouldn't say anything, lest Crimson went after Rey's sword too. "I don't think that's necessary. If you tell me not use it during the contest, I won't."

"Unfortunately, the school board doesn't trust you," Crimson said. "We would rather you left the sword with us until after the contest."

I frowned. This was bullshit. I was sure there was another reason behind it. What the hell did Crimson want my sword? "I just don't—"

"Erin," Crimson interrupted me, his voice tight. "I don't think you get it. Hand over the Dawnblade right now, or there will be consequences."

I crossed my arms, daring to defy him. Not because I wasn't afraid of the power he exerted as the headmaster, but because I hated him. "Like what?"

Crimson stood up and leaned over the desk, splaying both his hands over several loose sheets of paper. "Like expelling you and firing Professor Rey."

I felt the blood drained from my face. Holy shit, of course he would play this card.

I truly hated him.

Without a choice, I extended my arm beside me and summoned my Dawnblade. I held the hilt tight, then brought it up and handed it to Crimson.

My stomach revolved when he put both his hands around my sword and picked it up. His eyes shone bright. "It's beautiful." Holding the sword with one hand, he picked up a wooden box from underneath the desk and set it right in front of him. He opened it and placed the sword inside the black-velvet-lined box.

"What is that?" I asked, hating to see my sword tucked away.

"A protective case, so you can't call it again." He closed the box with a definite thump and glanced at me. "You can go now."

I hesitated. For a few seconds, I didn't move.

But I forced one foot in front of the other and exited his office. As I raced down the stairs, angry and with my pride hurt, I promised myself that I wouldn't leave it like that. Once the Shadow Trials were done, I would find a way to take my sword back.

16

WHEN ERIN TOLD me Crimson had taken her Dawnblade, I almost flipped. If I had had my way, I would have marched to his office and beaten the Dawnblade from him. But Erin assured me she was okay.

"You'll only buy us more trouble if you beat Crimson up," she pointed out.

True.

So we focused on the matter at hand. During the week, Erin kept on trying to use the map, but it didn't fucking work. She even called Harper's grandmother, and the old woman said the map should be working fine. Maybe Erin wasn't relaxed enough to do the spell, the old woman said, which only made Erin more stressed.

So I came up with a plan. If Erin found out about it, she would kill me.

I told her I had a staff meeting on Friday night, but I went back to the club instead.

The club owner told us Jasmin left the club with different men each night she went there, so I was hoping she would be there tonight, and I would be that man. Once she invited me out, I would talk to her about the mark on her wrist.

Something told me Jasmin looked for attractive men, so I put on fitted black pants, a dark gray shirt, and combed my hair back. I even folded the sleeves of my shirt to my elbows, knowing women liked that.

Then, I sat by the bar, ordered a beer, and waited.

Fortunately, it didn't take long for her to show up. Wearing a tight and short black dress and huge black heels, Jasmin strolled across the dance floor. The crowd parted, letting her pass as if she was a model in the catwalk. They all stared at her, ensnared in her web.

I had to admit, she was beautiful. Probably a little older than me, but tall, with nice curves, luscious red hair, and big red lips. As she approached the bar, I noticed her eyes were light hazel, almost as bright as Erin's. Her nose and chin were similar to Erin's too.

A couple of stools from me, she leaned into the bar. A bartender popped out of nowhere, already with a drink in hand. She smiled at him, and the man practically swooned.

What was up with her? Yes, she was pretty, but Erin was pretty too. Prettier, even, and men didn't drool after her like this. Or did they? No, I would have noticed.

Men flocked around Jasmin, trying to talk her, take her dancing, buying her drinks. My competition for the night was strong, and I felt fucking bad about approaching her. It felt like cheating on Erin, even though I didn't plan on doing anything like that.

I stayed in my seat for a while, just observing. The men came to her, but they also left after a while, as if she commanded them to. Was she some kind of demon with mind control?

Wary, I waited until she sent two of them away, and only one remained. Then, I switched stools, sitting right beside her.

"Good evening," I said over the loud music.

Jasmin turned to me, her smile wide. "Hello there." She ran her eyes over me. When her gaze met mine again, she licked her lower lip. "I'm Jasmin."

"I know," I said, turning my charm on.

She faked a shock. "You do?"

"Of course, everyone here knows who you are." I leaned in closer and said, "I bet half the males who are here came just to see the beautiful Jasmin."

She batted her lashes at me. "Did you come here to see me?"

"I did," I told her.

Her tongue snaked out and she licked her lower lip again. "What's your name?"

"Rey," I told her.

"What do you think if we get out of here, Rey?"

Whoa, that was fast. "I would like that."

She offered me her hand. "Come with me."

I took her hand and felt her magic wrapping around me.

Oh, I knew what she was.

Her magic was strong, but I was able to fight it off. I pretended to be entranced in her as she led me out of the club, into a cab, and to a small chalet in the mountains just outside of town.

Without ceremony, she entered her chalet, took off the jacket she had put on once we left the club, and brought me to the center of the open living room.

She stared at me, her hazel eyes turning black. "Kneel," she ordered, her voice turning guttural.

I exhaled. "You're a siren." I had encountered only a few sirens in my long lifetime, but they were all the same: They needed to kill males in order to keep their magic strong. "I'm a half-demon, so your spells won't work on me."

Shocked, she pulled back her magic and her eyes went back to normal. "I confess, it's rare when I find a man who doesn't succumb to my spell." She took a step back, until she was beside a low table. "But I do have a plan for when that happens." She opened the thin drawer under the table and pulled out a silver dagger. "I have to kill them anyway."

Dagger poised above her head, she lunged at me.

I sent a small darkfire bolt at her. It hit her hand, making her drop the dagger. She bent down to pick it up.

"I wouldn't do that if I were you," I warned, holding a bigger darkfire bolt in my hand.

She straightened and faced me. "What the hell do you want?"

I pointed to her wrist. "That mark. Do you know what that means?"

"Oh, I know." She stared at the mark. "Do you?"

I nodded. "I know other women with that mark."

"Oh, so you know Brikan, the king of the underworld, is my father. My poor mother didn't know who he was when she tried seducing him. He pretended to be entranced in her spell, and then he was the one to entrance her."

I frowned. "Where is she now?"

"My mother? Dead. She died when I was young, defending me against a demon." She rubbed a finger over the mark. "She told me this damn mark made me a demon kissed queen. It would attract demons, but once I figured out how to use my siren magic, I would be able to hide from them."

"You mean, you're untraceable?"

"It's like a switch. I can turn it on and off."

Then that was why Erin couldn't find her on the map anymore. "All right, I don't have time to go in circles. I know the other two Demon Kissed Queens. Together, the three of you can defeat King Brikan."

Her nose pinched. "Why would I want to defeat him? I don't even know him. As long as he doesn't bother me, I don't want anything with him."

"The Demon Kissed Queen prophecy says you three will rise and defeat him, taking control of the underworld. Do you think he'll just sit down on his throne and wait for you to come kill him? For all he knows, this prophecy is certain, and he'll try to stop it before it starts. Soon, he'll come for all of you, and he'll kill you before you grow strong together. That's why you have to do it *now*."

"And what do I gain from that?"

I blinked. "What?"

"I don't do things just because," she said, sounding bored.

"Brikan's biggest plan is to control the demon hunters so they can kill the other supernaturals, and then themselves. The world will become a dark, evil place. Saving the world from Brikan's wrath isn't enough?"

She shrugged. "I don't really care about that."

"What do you care about?"

She tapped her chin. "Money, jewels, power. That kind of stuff."

Of course, this wouldn't be fucking easy. One of Erin's sisters had to be a greedy bitch. "All right, I have a bargain for you. If you help us and if we win, I'll buy you a big diamond necklace. How about that?" I hadn't even given a present like that to Erin yet, but here I was, offering it to another woman. Hopefully, Erin would understand.

She scoffed. "I do like diamonds, but I want more."

I frowned. "What do you want?"

"I don't know. Surprise me."

I thought for a minute. This wouldn't be fucking easy, would it? Then I had an idea. "If you join us, I'll let you take a part of the underworld for yourself. You can rule it any way you want." I didn't want to think about the consequences of my bargain, not to mention how mad Erin would be with me once I told her what I had promised Jasmin. "What do you say?"

Jasmin smiled at me. "It's a tempting offer. I need time to think about it."

"We don't have time!" I was losing my patience.

"I don't care what you think, Rey. Just leave a phone number. I'll contact you once I make my decision."

I curled my hands into fists, trying to contain my anger. Why was she being so difficult? I forced myself to let out a long breath and calm down, because getting mad and yelling or fighting with her wouldn't get me anywhere. I couldn't force her to accept this.

I didn't have a choice here. I had to walk away and give her time to think about my deal.

"All right," I said with a sigh. I gave her my number, and she entered it in her phone. I also gave her Erin's number, just in case. "I'll be waiting for your call."

"Don't hold your breath," she said with a wink. She went to the front door and opened it for me.

Without another word, I walked out of her house.

17

ERIN

I THOUGHT Rey would come see me after his meeting Friday night, but he didn't. At one point, I even teleported to his house, but he wasn't there. This damn meeting was taking way too long.

Around midnight, I went back to my dorm, and even though I tried staying awake, I ended up falling asleep. It was mid-Saturday morning when I woke up to a knock on my door.

I rolled in my bed, annoyed. If it was Rey, I wouldn't be, but he wouldn't be knocking on my door inside the female dorm. Nope, he would first send me a text or call me. I glanced at my cell phone.

There was just one text from him sent at three in the morning.

Rey: *The meeting went on for hours. I don't want to bother you now. I'll call you tomorrow morning.*

I thought Crimson wasn't that close to Rey anymore. Why would a staff meeting last so long?

The knock came again.

"What the hell," I muttered, sitting up in bed. "I'm coming!"

Rubbing my eyes, I dragged my feet to the door. I opened a crack, but like a tornado, Ava pushed in and walked into my bedroom. I groaned. "Good morning to you too."

"It's not a good morning," she said. "Not for you, at least. You better sit down."

I stared at her. She looked pristine and energetic in a tight jeans pants and fitted pink sweater. Her blond hair fell down like a cascade on her back, still a little damp from a shower.

"Why?"

She pointed to the chair in front of the desk. "Just sit down, Erin."

I rolled my eyes, but relented. "What is it?"

She started pacing before me. "I went back to the club last night."

I frowned. "You mean, the club Rey took us to?"

She nodded. "Yup. I exchanged numbers with a guy I met that night, and he asked me to meet him." She waved her hands. "That's not important."

"You're getting on my nerves, Ava. What the hell is important, then?"

She stopped and faced me, her face grave. "I saw Rey there."

I blinked. "W-what?"

"He was flirting with a woman. And ..." She pressed her lips tight. "He left with her."

The floor opened and I fell into an endless dark pit. "W-what?"

"I'm sorry," Ava said in a low voice. "I almost came to wake you up when I got back in the middle of the night, but I was unsure if I should tell you or not. I was afraid you would be mad at me. Though, after I thought about it, I realized that if our roles were switched, I would have liked you tell me." She slapped her hands on her hips. "So here I am."

A slow dagger pushed through my heart.

No, this couldn't be right. After all we went through, Rey lied to me about a meeting and went back to the club? And he left with a woman? My stomach knotted and I felt sick.

No, this couldn't be true.

"A-are you sure?" I asked, my voice barely a whisper.

Ava nodded. "I'm sorry."

I bottled up the sadness and pain flooding me, and focused on anger. I was pissed. Furious. Suddenly, I shot up from the chair.

"He's dead," I said through gritted teeth.

Then I teleported to his townhouse.

I appeared in his bedroom, where he was sleeping in his bed, wearing black pajama pants and no shirt, a thin blanket knotted at his feet. For a moment, I wavered, because holy shit, he looked too damn hot and all I wanted was to curl up in bed with him.

But apparently, he had curled up in bed with someone else last night.

Another jolt of pain coursed through my chest and I felt breathless.

I picked up one of his boots from the floor and threw it at him. "Wake up, you jerk!"

The boot landed on his side and Rey suddenly sat up, blinking away the sleep. "What is it? What happened?"

I picked up the other boot and threw it at him. "You ... bastard."

He deflected the boot with his arm and stood from the bed. "Erin, what the fuck is going on?"

"You tell me!" I reached for a book over the dresser. "How was last night? The meeting was so boring, you decided to go find some fun somewhere else?"

His eyes widened. "What ... how do you know?"

More anger coiled in my belly and I threw the book at him. "So you admit it? You admit you cheated on me?"

He frowned. "Wait, what?"

"Ava saw you leaving the club with a woman, Rey. You can't deny it." I picked up a small decorative bowl. "Why did you do that?"

I aimed the bowl at him, but before I could let it go, Rey rushed me. In a flash, he was right in my face, holding my wrist with his big hand. "I didn't do anything."

"Bullshit! Ava saw you."

He got the bowl from me and set it down, but he didn't let go of my wrist. "Yes, I left with a woman. Jasmin. I was trying to get her alone so I could talk to her."

My shoulders sagged. "What?"

"You heard the club owner. She shows up there and always leaves with a man. So I tried playing that part."

"Why didn't you tell me?"

"Because I didn't think she would approach me if you were with me, and ... because I didn't think I would be able to fake-flirt with her with you watching me, and I didn't want to worry you about it. But I did plan on telling you about it first thing when I saw you today."

I stared at him, at his clear gray eyes, at his handsome, rugged face. "So, you left with her." My stomach tightened again. I had seen with my own eyes that Jasmin was a beautiful woman, and Rey had flirted with him. Fake-flirted, whatever. Still, that didn't sit well with me. "What happened then?"

"She's a siren," he said. "A siren needs to feed off the energy of males to survive. That's why she always leaves the club with a new man each night."

"Did she try to kill you?"

"She did, but her spells don't work with me. Instead, I told her why I was there."

"And?"

"She knows what the mark means and who her father is," Rey continued. "But she has no interest in joining us."

Another one? I understood if Kristin didn't join us; after all, she was young. But Jasmin? She was older than me. She could certainly participate in the upcoming war. "So that's it? She just won't come?"

"She seems to want power without much trouble, so I ended up offering her something. A piece of the underworld to rule if—*when*—we win."

"I don't want any piece of the underworld. She'll have to decide that with Tanner and the others." I frowned. "What did she say?"

"That she would think about it. I left our numbers for her."

I groaned. "Hopefully, she won't take long to come to her senses and agree to it."

"So you're okay with it?"

I lifted my chin, still a little hurt. "With what? You sneaking into a club without my knowledge? Leaving with another woman? Going to her house? Nope, I'm not okay with it."

"Erin ..." Rey reached up with his other hand and ran his fingers across my cheek. "I was just trying to help. I have no interested in Jasmin or any other woman. Only you." He took another step, erasing the distance between us. I inhaled deeply. "You know you're the only one for me."

"Don't," I whispered. "I want to give you hell for lying to me."

He leaned into me, his mouth so close to mine. "You're my soulmate, Erin. I love you too fucking much, and nothing will ever change that."

Holy shit ...

My anger faded. Suddenly hot and bothered, I rose on my tiptoes and brushed my lips to his. Capturing my mouth with his and deepening the kiss in a matter of seconds, Rey pushed me back, against the dresser.

In no time, our clothes were on the floor and we were in his bed, our bodies tangled and our hearts beating as one.

"So, what do we do now? Just wait?" Erin asked, her head against my chest.

"I guess so," I said, running my hand up and down her smooth back, glad she wasn't mad at me anymore. I had every intention of telling her about Jasmin today, but the blond bitch beat me to it. Thankfully, Erin understood what I had done and why I had done it.

"What if she takes months to make up her mind?"

"Then I guess we just hope Brikan doesn't attack us until then."

Erin lifted her head. She crossed her arms on my chest and rested her chin on her hands, looking into my eyes. "Meanwhile, we just keep going to classes and praying the damn Shadow Trials are canceled?"

"That and ..." There was something that had been bothering me since it happened. "We can investigate Tom's death."

Erin frowned. "Crimson isn't doing a good job?"

"I think Crimson isn't doing anything, actually," I told her. "Even if he was, I don't think he knows Tom was possessed. I can only guess the demon who possessed him also killed him."

"So, you want to find the demon?"

I nodded. "Yes. I want to know why it possessed Tom and why he killed his host. I want to know if this demon has possessed someone else and will soon kill another student, or if he's after you, just like Orzon was."

"And knowing you, you want to go now?"

"Well, it's almost noon, so we should have lunch first." I ran my hand through her long hair. "But no, not now." Being Saturday, the students were probably around campus, even if it was to and from the gym or the library. Walking among them would be less suspicious; however, Erin and I wouldn't be able to investigate together. "Later tonight, after curfew." Then the guards and patrols would be out, but with Erin's teleporting spell, we could easily sneak around them.

Erin reached for her cell phone on the nightstand. "That means we still have about ten, maybe eleven hours to kill. What do you want to do?"

Was that even a question? With a half smile, I flipped us around, trapping her under me. Erin half-gasped, half-moaned when I pressed my body to hers. "I think we can come up with something."

IT WAS ALMOST midnight when Erin teleported us to the Orchid building, where Tom was killed—or at least, where his body was left.

Careful to stay out of sight of the windows and glass doors, Erin and I walked down the hallway with a small orb of darkfire serving as light. We stopped right where his body was found, but there was nothing there to tell us the story. The blood from the floor and walls had been removed, and I couldn't sense the use of demon magic. Either Tom had been killed by a normal demon hunter, or this demon was strong.

Erin knelt on the hard, cold floor. "One of the dark spells my mother taught me during break was to track demons."

I frowned. Darkfire was a weak kind of dark magic. The kind of dark magic Martha had been teaching Erin was absolutely the worst. "Erin, I would rather you don't rely on dark magic."

"I won't rely on it," she said. "I haven't done any dark magic spells since we came back to the academy."

Still, I didn't like it, but I knew that urging her to not use it would only make her want to use it more. So, I stayed quiet and watched as she touched the floor and closed her eyes.

A moment later, her eyes snapped open, completely black.

I inhaled sharply, not liking this at all. "What is it?"

"I can sense him," she said, her voice eerie. She blinked and her dark eyes were gone. She stood and offered her hand to me. "Come with me."

Erin teleported to the forest outside the academy, right in front of a cave opening—the same one where the portal to the underworld was once located. "The demon is here?"

A cold wind blew past us and Erin rubbed her hands together. "Yes. Inside the cave."

I stared at the dark cave. "Why would the demon be hiding here?"

Erin shrugged. "Maybe it's waiting until it can possess someone else? I don't know."

"Then let's go ask him." I extended my hand, ready to summon my Dawnblade, but stopped myself. I didn't want to go flaunting my sword around while Erin didn't have hers anymore. Instead, I conjured a strong bolt of darkfire.

Erin did the same, and we entered the cave together.

Our darkfire illuminated the way as we went in, but we stopped after a few steps, because right in the center of the large cave was a higher demon.

In his human form, the demon was kneeling on the floor, his arms stretched to the sides in a dark, magical rope, and his head hanging low.

"Is he dead?" Erin asked in a whisper.

"I'm not dead," the demon replied, his voice brittle.

Bringing my darkfire higher, I took two steps closer. "What happened to you?"

The demon lifted his head. He looked like a man, except for his pitch-black eyes and his razor-sharp teeth. "Wouldn't you like to know," he rasped, trying to laugh.

Erin marched over, bringing her arm up. She closed her hand in the air and squeezed. Her dark magic wrapped around the demon's neck. Gasping, he stared at her with wide eyes.

"Did you possess a student from the Blackthorn Hunters Academy?" she asked. "Did you kill the student?" She eased her grasp on him a little.

The demon inhaled deeply before answering. "I possessed him, yes, but I didn't kill him. In fact, I was able to get away just in time." He snorted. "Only to be caught a moment later and be imprisoned here."

"By whom?" I asked. "Who killed the student? Who did this to you?"

The demon shook his head. "I can't say."

"What do you mean, you can't say?" Erin asked. "Tell us, or I'll kill you."

"I'm already dead," the demon said, his voice breaking. "The demon who captured me is much, much stronger than I am."

This demon was a higher one, I could sense it, even if I couldn't tell exactly what kind of demon he was. And he was afraid of whoever did this to him.

"Who was it?" I asked. "Was it a prince?" I paused, not really happy with my next question. "Was it Brikan?"

Erin's head whipped to me, her eyes wide.

"I—" The demon's eyes widened and his mouth fell open, as if he was being strangled.

I turned to Erin, but her arms were relaxed. She wasn't the one doing this. "What the fuck?"

Erin brought her hands up. She grabbed the air and pulled her hands apart, as if she was stretching a tight rubber band. "I can't stop it," she said through clenched teeth. "This is too strong."

A sick crack echoed through the cave as the demon's neck broke. His head lolled forward, and his body sagged against the magical ropes.

I grabbed Erin's hand. "Take us out of here. Right now."

Erin teleported us back to my townhouse, right in the middle of the empty living room. Her arms shook while I immediately started pacing.

"Something killed him," she whispered, staring at the wall behind me. "Something more powerful than him, more powerful than me, killed him right in front of us."

I halted. "It's like whoever killed him was listening to us. This demon or person or whatever doesn't want us finding out about him."

She shifted her eyes to me. "I think it was a demon," she

whispered. "When I tried prying the dark magic from his neck, it felt like a demon's."

I let out a long sigh. We hadn't solved anything. The demon was dead, and we didn't know why he possessed Tom or who killed him.

But more worrying was the fact that the higher demon was afraid of whoever killed him, which meant there was something even worse than a higher demon at the academy.

19

WITH THE SHADOW Trials hanging over our heads, the professors of every class started teaching us tricks and skills we might need during the deadly contest. Some of the demon hunter students complained about the changes in the curriculum, since they wouldn't be participating in the contest, but I was glad. Claire also seemed to be in heaven since she was learning new things.

During a Potion Making class, Professor Wesley took us around the campus, where it had been cleared of snow, and taught us about the kinds of herbs and moss that grew here, and into the forest. Some of these herbs could be substituted for other ingredients used in major spells. He even scraped a nasty looking moss from the roots of a seemingly dead tree, mixed it with water and some other common herbs, and created a healing paste.

"This won't heal a fatal wound," he said, showing us the thick paste. "But it'll heal small to moderate ones. It'll also stop the bleeding and prevent infection."

I frowned, wondering how bad this contest was going to

be if he was teaching us how to create a healing potion on the go. I was starting to get really nervous about the damn Shadow Trials.

Claire, Harper, and I went around the trees, looking for the herbs and roots listed on a list we had received in class. Though I was doing the work, my mind wasn't in it. I kept thinking about the demon who had possessed Tom and then was killed right in front of my eyes, by something I couldn't see. It had been a few days ago, but I couldn't forget what happened. Nor did I want to. Rey and I had talked a lot about it. If that demon was afraid of whatever killed him, we should be too.

But what was it? Where did we find it?

Rey told me not to worry about it, but I knew that after we parted ways in the middle of the night, he didn't go back to bed. I knew he searched the academy for this *thing*.

I didn't like it, but I knew that asking him to stop wouldn't work. So, I pretended I didn't know anything. I was sure that if he found something, he would let me know. Depending on what it was, he would even ask my help dealing with it.

But honestly, I hoped he didn't find it. I didn't want him to find it, because whatever it was, I was sure we weren't ready to deal with it.

"That's the wrong one," Claire said, pointing at my plastic bowl.

I stared at it. "Oh, damn it."

"Where's your head at?" Harper asked, coming to our side.

"Ugh, everywhere?" I joked, though it wasn't a joke. I dumped the wrong herb on the ground.

Claire put some of her herb in my bowl. "Do you want to talk about it?"

"Not here." I glanced around, to all the students close by. "Besides, you guys know." I had told them about Kristin, Jasmin, Tom's possession, the demon, and whatnot. Was I missing something? I didn't think so.

"We can talk more tonight, then." Harper winked at me before pointing to another herb on our list.

Claire followed her, and I stayed a few steps away on purpose. It was clear that Harper was flirting with Claire, though Claire was clueless. Just the other day, she mentioned how hurt she still felt because of Tanner and the demon who had possessed him. I didn't think she would be open to a new relationship, which actually made me sad. I wished to see Claire and Harper happy together.

We gathered the damn herbs, until a couple of guards approached Professor Wesley. I stopped and watched as the guards said something to the professor then left.

Professor Wesley turned to us and said, "Attention, everyone. We were summoned to the courtyard. The headmaster has an important announcement."

He spun around and marched toward the courtyard. The entire class followed him.

On the way, I glanced at Claire. "Do you know anything about this?"

She shook her head. "I have no idea."

Well, whatever it was, we were about to find out.

20

REY

I HAD SEARCHED for the demon, or whatever, all week, but had no fucking luck. Whatever it was, it was good at hiding. Besides that, Erin and I waited for Jasmin's call, the one that never came.

Now that she had found the other two Demon Kissed Queens, Erin didn't have much to do other than wait for them to join her. But would they come? Kristin was too young, and Jasmin seemed uninterested.

If they didn't come, if they didn't join us, we were doomed.

Then there was Fiona. We had lost hope of finding her for now. All we could do was wait for Tanner to find her for us.

Other than that, life at the academy went on. I taught classes, Erin went to classes, and at night, we spent as much time together as we could.

On Friday morning, I noticed Harvey didn't pay attention to anything I said during class. He reminded me of Erin last semester, when she sat through my class but purposely ignored everything I said. This time, though, I thought Harvey wasn't doing it on purpose.

When the time ended, I dismissed class. Harvey was so out of it, he didn't move until I called him.

"What?" He glanced around, just now seeing all the students filing out of the classroom. "Shit, I zoned out again." He picked up his books and dragged his feet toward the door.

"Harvey," I called. He turned to me. "What's going on?"

He shrugged. After all the students were gone, he approached my desk. "Nothing."

I knew that was a lie. Yesterday, I had seen him staring at Ava like a creeper. Something was going on there. "It's about Ava."

He groaned. "Yeah, it is. She has been going out with a guy she met at the club. Or rather some demon."

"And you don't like it."

"Of course I don't like it," he snapped.

"You're jealous, which means you like her, you dumbass."

"I know." He groaned again. "I was such a jerk. I wasn't even sure how I felt about her until I saw her paying attention to some other guy." He clenched his fists. "I hated that."

"Advice from a friend: You better hurry up and make up your mind, before another guy makes it up for you and sweeps Ava off her feet. Once her heart is gone, it's gone."

"I know, man, I know. I've been thinking about this for days now. I want to talk to her, but it feels like I already missed my chance."

I shook my head. "It's not too late. Look at Erin and me. We broke the soul bond and I kept pushing her away, and she still took me back when I finally confessed."

Harvey snorted. "You two are soulmates, man. Ava and I are not."

"Says who?"

Harvey narrowed his eyes, thinking.

Loud chatter and steps came from the hallways, drawing our attention to the classroom door. Harvey and I spied out and saw students and staff milling out of the building.

"What's going on?" Harvey asked.

A second later, Professor Ivan appeared by our side. "The headmaster is calling everyone to the courtyard. He's going to make an announcement."

I frowned. "Did you know about that?"

Ivan shook his head. "No, this is the first I'm hearing about it."

What the fuck was Crimson up to?

Harvey and I joined the others and exited the building. The courtyard was already half full of students and staff shivering in the cold weather.

I caught sight of Erin on the other side of the courtyard with Claire and Harper. Soon, Ava joined them.

It didn't take long for Crimson to step out of the Aster building and address the crowd.

"Thank you all for stepping out of your classes to hear my announcement," he said, sounding a little excited.

I wondered if he was going to talk about Tom's death. He hadn't mentioned anything about it since he told us he would be investigating it himself. Had he found the culprit? Would he tell us about who it was? Would he have drawn a crowd for that?

Harvey crossed his arms. "This should be good."

"We've been all waiting for the Shadow Trials, which were first scheduled for the end of the semester," Crimson said, his voice loud, carrying across the courtyard. "I decided to move up the date of the contest. The Shadow Trials will start tomorrow."

My jaw fell open and my stomach dropped. "What the fuck is he saying?"

Harvey slapped my arm. "Language, man. The students will hear you."

But nobody would hear me because they were all busy either celebrating (the demon hunters) or protesting (the half-demons) about it. The voices grew louder, calling Crimson names not even I had heard before. A brawl started in the center of the crowd, probably of demon hunters and half-demons who were arguing about the contest.

I glanced at Erin. She seemed as shocked as I was, staring at Crimson as if she hadn't heard him right. I knew that feeling.

"Attention!" Crimson shouted, his voice carrying over the courtyard. The crowd quieted a little. "This isn't up for discussion. Because of the contest, we're canceling the rest of the classes for today. Half-demons, use this time to rest and get ready." He offered a fake smile to his students. "I'll see you all in the arena behind the Hyacinth Building tomorrow evening."

With that, he simply spun around and marched into the Aster building.

Another brawl started, followed by more shouting and arguments. The professors pushed through the crowd, trying to break up the fights, and telling everyone to go back to their dorms.

Near us, Professor Ivan ran around like crazy, escorting students out of the courtyard. Meanwhile, Professor Coyne stared at the crowd from afar with an amused grin. Sometimes, I thought he liked this—the mess, the fight, the blood.

I remembered seeing him smiling like that when Tom was killed. I bet he would enjoy the Shadow Trials. The guy was fucking sick.

"What are you going to do?" Harvey asked, a glint of worry in his eyes. "You have to participate, right?"

I nodded. "I do, but nobody knows it yet." I inhaled deeply. "I guess that will be another big surprise."

SINCE THE STUDENTS and professors had been dismissed for the rest of the day, I invited Erin to come to my townhouse. I didn't know what to expect of the Shadow Trials, and I just wanted to have a nice time with her before this fucking contest started.

She said she would spend the afternoon with her friends, which made me a little jealous, but I understood. I took that time to organize everything. I made sure my bedroom and bed were clean, and started dinner.

When Erin arrived a little past six in the evening, I was finishing the spicy mustard sauce that would go with the steak. I glanced at her and my heart skipped a beat. She wore a simple black sweater and jeans, and her hair was loose around her shoulders. Nothing out of the ordinary, but still so fucking beautiful.

She took a long sniff and smiled at me. "What are you up to?"

I shrugged, stirring the sauce. "Just thought we could have a nice meal together."

She walked to me, embraced me from behind, and rested her head on my back. "I like that."

She stayed like that while I checked on the steak in the

oven, and when I grabbed the plates from the cabinet. She shuffled with me whenever I moved.

I lowered the heat of the saucepan and turned to her. "What is it?"

She glanced up at me, her chin on my chest. "Let's run away."

"What? Where is that coming from?"

"I'm serious," she said, pulling back a little. "My sisters won't join us, which means we'll be weak against King Brikan. We can't find Fiona. And there's the Shadow Trials tomorrow. Our future looks bleak right now. We should run."

I pulled her back to me and kissed her forehead. "I'll confess it's tempting, but we can't. There's nowhere we can hide that King Brikan won't find us. Besides, do you really want to run and hide for the rest of your life? Always living in fear and looking over your shoulder?"

"Well, no, but what is the other option? Stay here and die?"

I ran my hand through her hair. "First, we stick together and survive the Shadow Trials tomorrow. Once that's behind us, we'll focus on defeating the supreme demon. We'll find some other way," I said, trying to convince not only her, but me too.

"I'll pretend I believe you."

I smiled at her. "You better."

She glanced to the range. "So, is this food ready or not?"

I slapped her gently. "Go sit that pretty little ass, and I'll bring the perfect feast for you."

She raised her eyebrows at me. "Is the perfect feast you? Otherwise, it's not perfect."

The glint in her golden eyes, the faint purr in her voice,

the way she shifted her hips to the side ... was she kidding me?

I turned off the sauce and the oven and advanced on her. "If we eat dry, burnt steak, it's all because of you."

She smiled as I crashed into her and slid my hands down her back. "I'm glad to take that blame."

I dipped into her, taking her mouth with mine.

Taking all of her.

Now and forever.

21

I DIDN'T SLEEP the previous night, and it wasn't because Rey had his hot, naked body pressed to my side. I was freaking nervous.

Today was the Shadow Trials, and something told me this deadly contest was going to be even worse than I first imagined.

I spent the morning with Rey, and then the afternoon with Claire and Harper. With the mood so tense, it felt like we were going to say goodbye.

When I was ready to go to the arena, Ava stopped by my room and wished me luck.

"You better come out of there alive," she said, sounding like the blond bitch she was.

At seven in the evening, all the half-demon students and the members of the Black Knight Army gathered at the arena behind the Hyacinth Building, dressed in our combat training clothes and thick coats. I had packed a few allowed supplies, like common herbs and bandages, in my pockets. Cell phones and weapons weren't allowed, however.

Meanwhile, the demon hunter students and staff watched from the bleachers. Here and there, there were shouted insults and wicked laughter, but overall, I knew the demon hunters were enjoying this. Soon, several of the half-demons would be dead. What else they could ask for?

A large table had been set up on one side of the arena, where the judges were seated: Crimson, Professor Ivan, and Professor Coyne. If I had to say, only Professor Ivan seemed like he cared. The other two would fail all the half-demons if they could.

I glanced around, looking for my soulmate. He said he would hold out until the last second, so as not to generate more arguments and fights among the students. Though, when he walked into the arena, dressed just like the other half-demons, and stood by my side, there was nothing we could do to stop the insults. Someone even threw an empty water bottle at Rey. Thankfully, it missed him.

Crimson rose from his chair behind the table. "My dear half-demons. You'll be dropped in the mountains, several miles from here. You are expected to overcome the obstacles you'll face there and make your way back here. Once you arrive in this arena, it'll look different. Then we'll have your last trial."

"Care to elaborate?" someone asked from among us.

"You'll find out soon enough," Crimson said.

Suddenly, a portal opened up. What the hell?

"Crimson has magic?" I asked Rey in a low voice. "How the hell did he do that?"

"Must be a witch." Rey glanced around, his eyes narrowed. "Either a witch is hidden nearby, or he bought a spell from one."

"Step through the portal," Crimson said, waving his hand

at the giant magical doorway. "Professor Genevieve will be waiting for you on the other side."

The half-demons started making their way through the portal.

Rey extended his hand to me. I raised my eyebrows at him. "Everyone will see it."

He shrugged. "I don't care." He slipped his hand into mine and squeezed tight.

Then we stepped through the portal into a wide, snow-cleared meadow.

As Crimson had said, Professor Genevieve was there, surrounded by torches that illuminated the place, directing us to stand around the clearing. Once we were all there, the portal closed. She repeated the words Crimson said about having to find our way back to the academy, and the final trial would be in the arena.

"Just take your time," she said. "Since you're all far from the academy and have no maps, we actually don't expect to see any of you back until tomorrow morning." She glanced at her wristwatch. "Just a minute more." I looked at my watch. It was almost eight already. Had the portal eaten time? "Ready?" She dropped her arm. "You may start now!"

The contestants looked around, a little lost on where to go. At night, we couldn't even use the sun to guide us.

"Where to now?" I asked Rey.

He looked up to the sky. "Give me a second."

"What are you doing?"

"Reading the constellations to know which way to go."

"You know how to read the constellations?"

He returned his eyes to me. "I'm almost a thousand years old, remember? I know *a lot* of things." He tugged at my hand and we started for the forest.

Professor Genevieve waved at us. "Good luck," she mouthed.

With a ball of darkfire floating over our heads, Rey and I disappeared among the trees, where a thin layer of snow covered the ground. And a bunch of half-demons either followed us, or happened to decide this was the best way to go.

"I don't like this," I muttered to Rey.

"Just ignore them for now, and keep moving." He glanced at the sky, through the leafless tree branches. "From what they say and my bearings, I do believe we're far from the academy."

Though we had the darkfire overhead, and it reflected on the white snow, I jumped with every little creak or crack in the night. My nerves were on fire, and I wasn't sure I would endure an entire night like this.

Still holding my hand, Rey stroked his thumb on my palm. "Just focus on us. On going forward. On getting back to the academy. The rest doesn't matter right now."

We trudged on for over an hour without any major incidents. I was starting to wonder if this would be it. We just had to march all night in the snowy, cold mountain, until we got to the arena tomorrow morning? Then what? We would be too tired to do whatever the last trial was? I didn't get it.

The crowd started thinning. They either slowed down, or walked past us, and soon, there was only a handful of groups close to us. Vaira, one of the first half-demons Rey recruited for the Black Knight Army, was among one of the biggest groups to our left. Still upset with Rey because he couldn't stop the Shadow Trials from happening, she ignored the both of us.

Suddenly, howls and growls filled the night.

We all stopped dead in our tracks as we listened.

The sounds were guttural, followed by shrieks and piercing cries. Sounds I had heard before. My eyes widened. "This is it. That's what I heard when I accidentally went to the dungeons."

"What?" Rey asked. "How do you know?"

The shrieks, the growls ... there wasn't anything else like them. "I just know."

Out of nowhere, a huge brown werewolf attacked the group to our right. The half-demons screamed and retreated, but one of them ended up underneath the wolf's paws and jaw. Red stained the snow as the wolf ripped the guy's throat.

My blood turned to ice.

"Holy shit," I whispered.

The werewolf turned to the others. A girl stepped forward, a bolt of darkfire in her hand. "Come at me, you stupid dog."

The wolf growled at her, foam gathered at its big mouth. Its dark eyes were unfocused, and it seemed rabid.

She threw the bolt at the wolf.

Four more werewolves appeared from the shadows.

Rey tugged at my hand. "Time to go." He started running, taking me with him.

I almost tripped on my own legs as I tried to process what was happening. Rabid werewolves were attacking us. This was a part of the Shadow Trials. The sounds I heard in the dungeons weeks ago had been these werewolves. Crimson had imprisoned them, and probably driven them crazy, and now he was letting them attack us.

This was just insane.

More supernaturals attacked the groups without mercy—

demons, vampires, fae, and even some weird looking foxes with multiple tails.

When a duo of demons dove for Rey and me, I blinked us several yards ahead. I could probably teleport us to the academy, or closer to it, but I was honestly afraid of what else we would find on the way, or at the academy. According to Crimson, the final trial would be the worst, which meant whatever he had planned was worse than this. I wasn't eager to face it.

A scream made me jump. I looked back and saw as a vampire lunged for Vaira. She tried using her magic to stop it, but she wasn't fast enough. The vampire bit her.

Then another one jumped for her. Then another. In less than a second, there were five vampires feeding from Vaira.

My stomach turned, and I felt like I was about to lose the snack I had eaten this afternoon.

Holding Rey's hand tight, I teleported us again, this time a longer distance, so we could take a breather.

"We can't keep running all night," Rey said.

"I can teleport us closer to the academy," I suggested. "Maybe we can hide somewhere. Oh, that cave where the demon was imprisoned."

Rey's brow furrowed. "I don't think staying there is a good idea."

I glanced around, trying to find another place to hide. Between the high moon, the snow, and the darkfire, the area around us was well-lit, but it was still a lot darker than if it was daytime, and I couldn't see far.

I didn't have time to react when a vampire rammed Rey with his super speed. The two of them went down in the snow and my heart stopped. Rey was faster and used his darkfire to push the vampire off him. Enraged, I ran at the vampire. He bared his fangs at me, but before he could do anything, I pushed my hand into his chest, sending my dark magic into him.

The vampire's dark eyes widened as my magic spread inside him, burning every inch of his body. In no time, the vampire fell back into the snow, completely still.

And I turned to Rey.

Groaning, he stood, his hand pressed to his shoulder and blood seeping between his fingers.

My heart squeezed. "You're hurt."

"I'll live," Rey said, through gritted teeth.

The howls and shrieks echoed through the night. We didn't have time to do anything other than run.

I held on to Rey and teleported us out of there.

ERIN TELEPORTED us a little farther ahead, then a little more, and a little more. Each time we stopped, she glanced around, looking for a place to hide. And I groaned. This jumping around wasn't helping with the fucking pain in my shoulder.

Thankfully, the vampire hadn't bitten me. He had scratched me with his long claws when brawling with me, but it was a fucking deep scratch and it burned more and more with each passing second.

Finally, Erin found a little cave probably halfway down the mountain. She helped me inside and down onto the cold stone ground.

Eyes shining with worry, Erin pried my fingers from the wound. "Shit," she muttered. "The bandages I brought won't be enough for this." She ripped the inside layer of her coat and tied it tight around my shoulder. I groaned, swallowing a cry as the pain intensified. "This should help with the bleeding." Then she got up.

"Where are you going?" I asked, my voice weak.

"To find an herb to help with healing," she said.

"An herb? In the snow?"

"Professor Wesley taught us how to find specific herbs hidden in the snow." She pressed her lips tight, her eyes on my shoulder. "I'll be right back."

I didn't know how long she was gone. At first, I tried staying awake and enduring the pain, but with the blood loss and everything else, my body caved and I ended up closing my eyes for a moment.

I woke up when Erin untied the cloth from around my shoulder and applied the herb directly to the wound. Pain shot down my arm and chest, and I gritted my teeth, doing my best to keep it together. She ripped another piece of cloth from her coat and tied it around my shoulder.

"It should at least stop the bleeding," she said, her voice carrying a worried lilt.

"I'll be fine," I said, though I didn't feel fine. How was I supposed to finish the fucking Shadow Trials like this?

Erin scooted close to me. "We should be fine here." She wrapped her arm around me and pulled me to her. "Let's just sleep and rest."

I tried resisting it again, but wasn't able to.

Pressed against Erin, I slept.

A BRIGHT LIGHT woke me up. When I finally opened my eyes, the sunlight was streaming inside the cave, bright and almost warm.

Erin lifted her head and glanced at me. "How are you feeling?"

I sat up and tried rolling my shoulders. Pain coursed down my arm again, but it wasn't as much as last night. And I didn't feel like lying back down and sleeping some more. "A lot better."

She offered me water from a small bottle, and a granola bar. Great breakfast, but better than nothing. I took a sip of water and forced myself to eat.

"Do you think you can keep going?" she asked, still worried.

I nodded. "I think we have no choice." I started getting up, but noticed Erin's forlorn eyes. "What is it?"

"We could still run away," she said, her voice low. "We're outside the campus; nobody knows where we are. We can just change direction and go."

I confess the offer was tempting, but we couldn't give up now. I wanted to believe there was still hope. That we would soon be finished with the Shadow Trials, that Jasmin would join us, that Karen would let Kristin come too, that we would find Fiona, and that we would defeat King Brikan in the end.

What I most wanted was to overcome all that and *then* leave everything behind. Take Erin with me and just live. Enjoy life. Spend all of our time together. Do nothing and everything. It didn't matter, as long as we were together.

"We're almost done," I told her.

"Didn't you see what happened last night? If that was the beginning of the trials, what's waiting for us at the end?" She shook her head. "I'm not sure I want to find out."

I cupped her face. My shoulder groaned in protest, but I swallowed the curse that rose to my tongue. "Nothing can defeat us when we're together. I'm sure it's going to be bad, but if anyone can defeat it, it's us."

Erin stared at me with those bright golden eyes. "I'm just ... tired of all of this. I want it all to end."

I slipped my hands down and entwined my fingers with

hers. "It will. I promise you, it will." Biting back the pain that shot through my body, I stood up and tugged on her hands, pulling her up with me.

Erin glanced at my shoulder again. "Are you sure you're okay?"

I nodded. "I'll live." I leaned into her and pressed a soft kiss on her lips. "Now let's go."

We walked out of the cave and blinked at the brightness of the day. The sun was high and uncharacteristically warm for this time of year, and the snow was bright with the sun's shine.

Slowly and aware, we started down the mountain. It didn't take long for us to see the damage from the previous night. Bodies of half-demons and supernaturals littered our path, staining the snow with fucking blood.

I didn't count the bodies, but I would have guessed at least two-thirds of the half-demons had lost their lives last night.

Since it was already mid-morning, Erin teleported us down the mountain in several jumps, until we could see the academy in the distance.

We were almost there.

Then we heard them. Growls and howls, all coming for us.

We glanced back and saw rabid werewolves, drool and foam lining their foul mouths.

I caught Erin's hand in mine.

She teleported us out of there.

And right into the center of the arena.

ERIN

For a moment, I thought I had brought us to a different place, but then I recognized it. The arena had changed a little. The running track and field in the center had now sunk into the ground, becoming a pit, with high walls and metal gates around it, while the bleachers remained on the ground level, looking down at us.

"What the ...?" I muttered, confused.

I glanced around. There were nineteen half-demons here, leaning against the arena's new wall, or seated on the sandy ground. But, like Rey and I, they were all either hurt, dirty, or starving.

Crimson's voice echoing through the arena startled me. "Erin Delman and Rey Lowe." I turned to where I knew he was. There he was, looking all mighty in his chair behind the judges' desk. I wanted squeeze his throat. I just didn't because my best friend was his daughter. "That makes twenty-one half-demons who survived the first part of the trial. I heard more are coming, so we'll wait for a few more minutes before starting the next phase."

I clenched my fists, angry about all he had done to us so far, and worried about what was next.

"Erin!"

I looked up and easily found Claire, Harper, Ava, and Harvey sitting together right in front of one of the bleachers.

"Are you okay?" Claire mouthed.

I nodded. I was as okay as one could be in this situation.

Rey and I sat down in the middle of the arena, and I checked his wound. As promised by the professor, the herb had stopped the bleeding and I could easily see the wound healing. As best as I could with the few things I had, I cleaned the wound, applied more of the herb to it, and tied a clean piece of cloth around his shoulder.

"You'll soon have no coat left if you keep doing that," he said, trying to joke.

I shrugged. "As long as you get better, I don't care."

He stared into my eyes, his eyes almost silver under the bright sunlight. "I'm starting to doubt my choice."

"What do you mean?"

"We should have run away," he said in a low voice. He pressed a hand to his chest. "Something in here tells me I'll regret it."

Oh, no, he couldn't doubt it now. If he did, then I would too. So, I decided to be strong enough to make him strong too. "Nah. Didn't you say we'll make it work? We'll make anything work, as long as we're together? I believe that."

He scoffed. "Liar."

"I'm not lying. I do believe it." That was true. "But sometimes I can be very wary and worried. That doesn't change the fact that I believe in you."

One corner of his lips tugged up.

Just then, a half-demon arrived. The young man shuffled

in the arena and promptly fell to his knees, his chest bleeding.

Guards appeared from the side gates and rushed to the half-demon. They carried him out of the arena. The gates closed with a definite thud. A chill ran through my body. I didn't want to think what would happen to that student.

Not five minutes later, three more half-demons arrived, all in better condition than the previous one.

Crimson tapped the microphone, almost giving me a heart attack. "I was informed all other half-demons perished during the first part of the Shadow Trials." I glanced around. There were only twenty-four of us. There had been at least a hundred before, if not more. And now we were down to less than a quarter. I pressed a hand to my stomach. "This next phase consists of two rounds. During the first round, you'll go against demons." He gestured to the gates along the arena. As if on cue, demons appeared behind the gates. They pushed, pulled, shrieked, sneered, all the while looking at us as if we were their favorite meal. "Lots of demons. Kill them all. Then, we'll start the second round." Crimson raised his hand high. "Start!"

The gates opened, and the demons swarmed the arena.

Rey held my hand. Together in the center of the arena, we watched as two half-demons were killed almost instantly.

"Stick together!" Rey shouted. "Pull back and fight together!"

A handful of half-demons heeded his advice and joined us in the middle, but two others tried to fight the demons by themselves. They were easily overrun.

The eighteen remaining half-demons closed a circle around Rey and me, their backs to us.

"What now?" one of them asked.

"Now, we fight," Rey said. He let go of my hand and conjured a big darkfire bolt. Joining the others in the circle, he threw the bolt at a muttmaug. The god-like demon crumbled to the ground with the hit.

I glanced around.

So far, the demons hadn't stop pouring from the gates. There were probably over a hundred of them already against twenty of us. Rey and the others threw bolts at them, making them stay away, for now. We wouldn't be able to hold them back like that forever.

Seeing the four bodies on the ground, I had an idea. A terrible idea, but it was an idea nevertheless. Knowing that if I raised the dead to fight I would make people warier and more afraid of me, I cast another spell, one they wouldn't be able to notice. I syphoned the last of the life force from the dead bodies, bringing more power and magic into me.

It filled my veins, humming inside me.

I stepped beside Rey and let it out. I threw one strong bolt of dark magic to test it out. The bolt hit a darkelth square in the chest, but the demon didn't fall to the floor. The demon disappeared in a cloud of dust.

A smiled tugged at my lips.

I raised my hands high, bringing up a ring of darkfire around us. I pushed the ring out, toward the demons. Without anywhere to run, the wave of darkfire swallowed the demons, turning them into dust one by one. When the darkfire reached the wall of the arena, I pulled back my power.

The arena went dead silent.

My knees trembled as if I had just run a marathon and couldn't take one step more.

Rey knotted his arm under my elbow. "Hey, there. I've got you."

Clearing his throat, Crimson stood. "Well, that was … something." He covered the microphone and said something to Ivan and Coyne, before continuing, "Time for the final challenge. In this round, the half-demons will have to fight each other."

"What the hell?" someone asked behind me.

Like a sick man, Crimson grinned at us. "The last five half-demons standing will be the champions."

WHAT THE FUCK? Last five?

"So, you did all this to have only five of us survive?" Carl, a half-demon who had been in my class, asked. He pointed at Crimson. "You never had any intention of letting us live, did you?"

Crimson shrugged. "I'm letting five of you live. Isn't that already too much?"

I curled my hands into tight fists, considering jumping over the wall and punching him square in the nose.

"I won't fight," Erin protested.

"If any of you refuse to fight, then all of you will die today," Crimson warned.

What the fuck?

Whispers started around the bleachers. Though I knew most demon hunters were against the half-demons, I also knew some of them didn't sign up for an extermination of this scale.

Before it could get worst, Crimson shouted, "Begin!"

Instantly, Carl turned to us, a darkfire bolt in his hand. "I don't want to die."

But as he said that, another student advanced on him and pierced a dagger into his chest. A fucking dagger? Where did he get that from?

The half-demons turned against each other, and I grabbed Erin's hand and pulled her out of the fray. There was nowhere to run, but if we could avoid the fight, then we would survive.

"This isn't right," Erin muttered as we watched the half-demons killing each other. "This shouldn't be like this."

"I totally agree," I whispered.

With four half-demons down, the remaining fourteen stopped. They talked among themselves, then turned to Erin and me.

"Shit," Erin said, squeezing my hand.

They advanced on us.

"We don't have to fight," I told them. I was ready to fight, but I would rather they didn't try that tactic. "If we all protest, they won't have any choice, but to let us all live."

"As if," a guy spat. He cast a darkfire bolt and threw it at me. I deflected it, sending it to the wall behind us.

Two other half-demons sent bolts at Erin. She raised a shield in front of her, which absorbed the darkfire.

Then she lowered the shield. "Please, let's stop—" Her words died and her eyes went wide.

A darkfire bolt struck her.

The blood drained from my body. "Erin!"

I turned to her and cursed under my breath when I saw the wound on the left side of her stomach.

Face suddenly pale, she gulped. "It's n-nothing."

Enraged, I turned to the other half-demons. "You're all fucking dead." I summoned my magic and conjured powerful bolts in my hands.

"Stop!" a new voice echoed through the arena.

25

EVERYONE WENT STILL.

Crimson shot up from his chair and glared at Coyne, who was standing by his side. "What's the meaning of this?"

"My master wants this fight to stop," Coyne said, his voice eerie.

"What? Your master?!" Crimson's face turned red, probably angry with the interruption.

"Yes, his master," Ivan said, standing up too.

Even from above the arena, his eyes met mine. And he changed. His body grew taller, thicker, making his clothes rip at the seams. His hair became longer, his eyes brighter. Horns sprouted from the top of his head, and his teeth elongated, becoming sharp fangs.

"King Brikan," Crimson whispered, his eyes wide, his hands shaking.

Chaos erupted.

Ivan—no, Brikan—jumped into the arena, while the students and staff screamed and ran away. A few professors attacked him, but he erected a dark magic barrier around the arena, keeping them all out.

And trapping us in.

My heart hammered against my chest.

King Brikan was here.

My father was here.

And he was here for me.

Summoning his Dawnblade, Rey pulled me back behind him. The other students ran to the gates, yelling for help. But the gates didn't budge, and nobody came to help.

Eyes still fixed on me, Brikan flicked his hand and the half-demons were pushed into the gates with a loud bump. Then they fell to the ground, like discarded dolls.

Slowly, Brikan advanced toward me. "My dear Erin," he said, his voice rough and deep.

Through the pain coming from the wound on my stomach, I held Rey's shirt and retreated a couple of steps.

Rey raised his sword. "Stay back!"

"My dear Erin," Brikan said with a sigh. He halted, but I knew it wasn't because Rey had told him to. "I confess I disguised myself as Ivan and came to the academy to kill you, but once I saw you, once I got to know you, and I saw how strong you are, I changed my mind." He offered a sharp smile to me. "I want you to come with me. I want you to help me rule the underworld. You belong there with me."

He couldn't be serious. "What about the prophecy?" I asked, trying to buy us some time.

"It doesn't matter," he said nonchalantly. "If you come with me, I'll pretend it never existed. I'll forget about your sisters."

Bile rose in my throat. Of course he knew about them. He

knew about it all, and yet, he had waited, letting us—me—become more desperate as the time went by.

The offer was tempting, but only for about four seconds. Then I came to my senses. This was the king of the underworld. He was pure evil. He said he wanted me by his side? I really doubted that. The moment I gave my hand to him, he would either kill me, or imprison and torture me. Another big lie was that he would leave my sisters alone. Even if I accepted his offer, he would end up killing them, because he was smart enough to know that, while they remained alive, there was still a chance for the prophecy to come true.

He extended his big, clawed hand at me. "Come with me, Erin."

"Never," I spat the words, knowing what they would bring.

His wrath and a big battle I had no chance of winning.

But instead, he shifted his smile to Rey.

"Rey Lowe, Reyan, son of Prince Asmodeus, a powerful half-demon, general of several legions of demons in the underworld." Brikan's voice gained a lilting tone. "I've got an offer for you too."

Two pillars of smoke appeared beside Brikan, one on each side. The smoke twirled around, taking shape and color, forming something.

Someone.

Two women—an older one, and a little girl.

Rey went still. "Mother, Mariah," he whispered, his eyes wide.

"Come with me, and I'll resurrect them," Brikan said. The two women opened their arms, as if expecting a hug from Rey.

Rey took half a step forward. I tugged on his shirt. "Rey."

He took another step. I held on to his arm. "You know he's lying, right? Rey?" I stepped to his side and looked at him. His eyes were dazed, his face slack. I glared at Brikan. "What did you do to him?"

"Nothing he didn't want." Brikan dipped his chin once.

Rey turned to me, his eyes on my face, but not seeing. Startling me, Rey threw his hands out, sending a darkfire bolt at me. It hit me square in my chest, pushing me back several feet. I fell on the hard, sandy ground, pain radiating from my back, down my butt, and legs. But other than that, the bolt hadn't been strong.

It had been meant to just push me away.

Groaning, I pushed up.

But by then, Rey was almost beside Brikan.

"Rey! No!" I screamed.

A portal opened up between them. Brikan offered me a wide smile before stepping in.

Then Rey went through, without looking back at me.

I rushed to the portal, but it closed before I could reach it.

The images of his mother and sister faded in the air, and the barrier around the arena fell.

And I screamed.

ERIN

THE SCREAM RIPPED through my throat, until I couldn't scream anymore. I stayed rooted in place, so completely lost.

The portal was closed. Rey was gone.

A pang cut through my chest.

"Erin!" someone called.

But I didn't turn to the voice. I didn't even move. I had to stay here, I had to figure out how to open the portal, how to get Rey back.

Claire appeared in front of me, holding my shoulders. "Oh, Erin." She pulled me into an embrace. "I was so worried." Harper, Ava, and Harvey were beside her, watching me with careful eyes. Claire pulled back and stared at me. "How are you holding up?"

Ava slapped her arm. "Rey was just taken. How do you think she's holding up?"

Claire's face fell. "I meant her wound."

I glanced down to my stomach. I had forgotten about the wound. Blood slowly seeped from the cut on my left side. As if seeing it triggered something in my brain, pain spread through my middle and my vision blurred.

"Whoa." Harvey stepped to my side and passed an arm under my shoulders. "Let's take you to the infirmary."

As we turned to one of the gates around the arena, I saw the bodies of the half-demons. That was when I remembered the chaos hadn't been only here. Coyne had stayed out the barrier with the other students and the staff.

"What happened?" I asked, my voice breaking. Pain shot through my body with each step we took, and my vision darkened some more.

"The students fled while the professors fought Coyne," Harper said.

"We tried to help them, but Coyne disappeared," Ava added. "We think he was either a demon in disguise, or he had been possessed."

"When the barrier broke, we jumped into the pit," Claire continued. "I guess the professors are now trying to calm down the students."

"I wouldn't be surprised if there's no classes tomorrow," Harper said.

Harvey scoffed. "Just tomorrow? I bet this semester will be shut down, just like the previous one."

I frowned. I didn't care about the academy or the students. All I wanted was to put a bandage over this wound, so I could do something about Rey. I had to find a way to open that damn portal again. I had to go after him.

We went up to the ground level, Harvey carrying most of my weight.

Claire patted my arm. "We're almost there."

I blinked, trying to stay awake, holding on to the little strength I still had, just a little longer ...

But I fell into the darkness.

"Erin?"

I fluttered my eyes open and found my mother peering down at me. "W-what's going on?" I tried sitting up, but pain shot through my midriff.

My mother put her hands on my shoulders and pushed me down. "You lost a bit of blood. Just rest."

I glanced around at the wide room and several empty hospital beds around me. I was in the school's infirmary. I frowned. "Why are you here?"

"Erin, you fainted two days ago," my mother said. "A lot has happened since then."

This time, I pushed through the pain and sat up. "Two days?" No, no … that meant Rey had been in Brikan's clutches for two freaking days. "I have to go."

"Go where?"

I swung my legs off the bed. "Find Rey."

My mother halted in front of me, all stoic and serious as always. "And where is that, exactly?"

I stared at her, getting mad at her for coming in and already being against whatever I did or said. "Just get out of my way."

"Erin, just listen to me." She let out a long sigh. "Brikan took Rey because he knew you would come for him. It's a trap. And once you're there, neither of you is getting out. You know that, right? You have to know that."

A helpless feeling filled my chest and a sob rose to my throat. I knew that. I really knew that. Right now, neither Rey nor I were as powerful as Brikan. If I went after him, we were both either dead or imprisoned.

I swallowed another sob. "But ... I can't just stay here and do nothing."

My mother stepped closer and wrapped her arms around me. "Don't worry too much about Rey. Brikan will keep him alive and well, because he knows that's the only way to lure you in." She smoothed her hand down my messy hair. "Besides, you have plenty to do here." She stepped back and handed me some clean clothes. "Get dressed and come meet me in the headmaster's office. We have a lot to talk about."

I DIDN'T JUST GET DRESSED. I tried to keep my mind blank, otherwise I would break down and cry and do nothing else. I went to my dorm room, took a shower, changed my clothes, and went to the cafeteria to get something to eat. Since I had left the Iris building, where the infirmary was located, I hadn't seen anyone—no students, no staff—and now the cafeteria seemed closed.

What was going on? Had the school really shut down because King Brikan had showed up? I didn't doubt it.

I raided the kitchen, grabbing an apple and a package of chocolate chip cookies, then headed to the Aster building. Munching on the apple, I entered the headmaster's office.

My mother was seated behind the desk.

She gestured to the chair across the desk. "Sit down."

Wary of this conversation, I took the seat. "What is it?"

"I'll get straight to the point. Since King Brikan made his big entrance, Crimson disappeared. Claire called him, but all he said was for her to run, so we're safe to assume the school was left without a headmaster."

I gasped. "You're the new headmaster."

She nodded. "I had a meeting with the Blackthorn Hunters yesterday, and I was appointed as the new headmaster."

"But ... there's no one at the academy."

"There are a few people, but most are out. I gave everyone a week off to recover from what happened," my mother said. "Though I'm not naive. I know not everyone will come back. It's okay, because we have more important matters to focus on."

I frowned. "What do you mean?"

My mother glanced at her phone at the desk. "They should be here any minute now." A moment later, a knock came from the closed door. "Come in."

The door opened, and Claire, Harper, Ava, and Harvey entered the room.

But that wasn't all. Behind them were Tanner, Karen, Katrina, Kristin, and Jasmin.

I rose to my feet, not believing my eyes. "You came," I whispered, eyeing Kristin and Jasmin.

"I was promised something in return," Jasmin said, staring at her long red nails.

"We're here because Kristin wouldn't shut up," Karen said, sounding upset with the situation. "She bothered us nonstop for weeks until we finally relented."

It didn't matter how and why; I was just glad they were here.

My mother stood and walked to my side. "Now the three Demon Kissed Queens are together. We can get ready to fight back and take the battle to the underworld."

I stared at her, my eyes wide. She wanted us to go to the underworld? So, when we were there, I could save Rey?

My heart squeezed.

I glanced at my new allies and my friends, my eyes filling with tears. Our army wasn't large, but it was still a pretty good one. If we fought with good intentions, if we dedicated our hearts to our cause, I was sure we would succeed.

We had to.

THE MOMENT I crossed through the portal, the spell broke.

I blinked, waking up as if I had been trapped inside my own body. I saw everything that happened, even when I threw a darkfire bolt at Erin and sent her flying.

A pain cut through my heart.

"What the fuck?" I turned around to go back, but the portal closed behind me.

What had I done?

My chest tight, I glanced around. I had been to the underworld a lot while I worked for Asmodeus, but I had never stepped foot inside King Brikan's castle. I spun around on the black stone path, surrounded by red, hot lava, its heat licking against my skin and making me uncomfortable, and faced the dark gray skies and the black palace. It was a huge thing that sprawled over the monotone landscape, with several pointy turrets that disappeared among gray clouds.

Lightning cut across the skies, illuminating the many demons that crawled in the shadows, most of them watching me, aware of my presence there.

This was not good.

"Welcome to the underworld, Reyan," King Brikan said, his hands spread wide beside him. "I hope you have a good time here."

I clenched my hands into fists. "You spelled me! You used me to get to Erin! This is a fucking trap!"

Brikan grinned at me. "Glad you know."

The motherfucker …

"Take me back right now," I demanded.

"Or what?" Brikan asked, sounding amused. "You'll fight me? Think you can win against me?" He tsked. "You know you can't. If I were you, I would be a nice little boy and behave."

"Or what?" I asked, repeating his words.

Brikan loomed over me and I pushed back my fear. In his true form, he was probably over seven feet tall and intimidating. "Or I'll torture you within an inch of your life. After all, I can't kill you if I want Erin to come get you."

I pushed my hands through my hair. What the fuck had I done? I had been spelled and hadn't been in control, but still … Now Erin would find a way to come to the underworld to save me, just as Brikan wanted.

We were doomed, but I wouldn't let him see how hopeless I felt. If anything, I would give him hell every second I could.

"So you'll throw me in a dungeon and torture me, right?"

"Actually, I'm planning on giving you one of my luxurious guest bedrooms," Brikan said. I shook my head. The king of the underworld had guest bedrooms in his castle? "And, to sweeten this deal, I'll offer you more: I wasn't joking about bringing your mother and sister back." He twirled his hand and the shadows appeared beside him again.

My mother and my sister.

Floating above the stone path, they stared at me, their eyes full of pain and sadness.

An invisible hand clutched around my heart and squeezed hard.

I frowned. This could be a trick, a way of keeping my mind busy so I didn't rebel. But I had to admit, I was curious. "How?"

"It's a complicated ceremony, and time consuming," Brikan said. "We can work on it together."

I didn't like this. I didn't like this entire fucking situation, but if I was going to find a way of escaping, I had to act like a good boy and behave. That meant going with whatever shit Brikan came up with.

I swallowed the disgust and fear. "Let's do it."

Brikan showed me his sharp-toothed smile. "Wonderful." He beckoned me forward. "Now come. We've got a lot to do."

He started toward the castle, the demons in the shadows following his every move.

I stared at him for a moment. This was a temporary situation. I would pretend to go with the flow, to work on the fucking ceremony that would bring back my mother and sister. I would behave and stay quiet. But my mind would be working. I would watch everyone and everything. I would learn every detail about this castle and the demons, and even Brikan, and I would find a way of escaping before Erin came to rescue me.

That was a promise.

But for now, I followed him into his black palace.

READY FOR THE last installment of Rey's and Erin's story? Then grab *The Infernal Curse* now!

THANK YOU

Thank you for reading *The Shadow Trials*!

Reviews are very important for authors. If you liked my book, please consider leaving a review on your favorite retailer and/or on goodreads, please!

You can get book 5 now:

The Infernal Curse

Don't forget to sign up for my Newsletter to find out about new releases, cover reveals, giveaways, and more!

If you want to see exclusive teasers, help me decide on covers, read excerpts, talk about books, etc, join my reader group on Facebook: Juliana's Club!

ABOUT THE AUTHOR

While USA Today Bestselling Author Juliana Haygert dreams of being Wonder Woman, Buffy, or a blood elf shadow priest, she settles for the less exciting—but equally gratifying—life as a wife, a mother, and an author. She resides in North Carolina and spends her days writing about kick-ass heroines and the heroes who drive them crazy.

Subscribe to her mailing list to receive emails of announcement, events, and other fun stuff related to her writing and her books: www.bit.ly/JuHNL

For more information:
www.julianahaygert.com

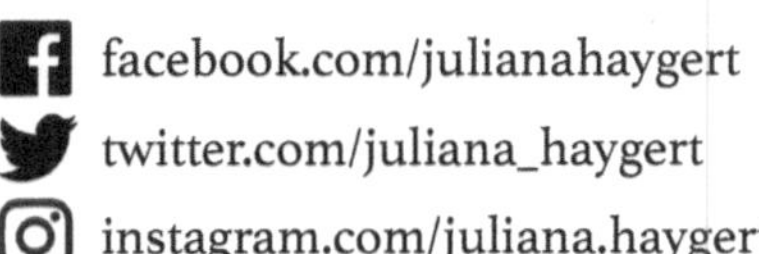

facebook.com/julianahaygert
twitter.com/juliana_haygert
instagram.com/juliana.haygert

ALSO BY JULIANA HAYGERT

To find links and more info, go to:

www.julianahaygert.com/books/

Shorts

Into the Darkest Fire

Tested

Rite World: Blackthorn Hunters Academy

The Demon Kiss (Book 1)

The Hunter Secret (Book 2)

The Soul Bond (Book 3)

The Shadow Trials (Book 4)

The Infernal Curse (Book 5)

Rite World

The Vampire Heir (Book 1)

The Witch Queen (Book 2)

The Immortal Vow (Book 3)

The Warlock Lord (Book 4)

The Wolf Consort (Book 5)

The Crystal Rose (Book 6)

The Wolf Forsaken (Book 7)

The Fae Bound (Book 8)

The Blood Pact (Book 9)

Breaking Away (Book 2)

Breaking Through (Book 3)

Breaking Down (Book 4)

<u>*Standalones*</u>

Daughter of Darkness